Harmless

J.C. Calkin

NEWMAN SPRINGS PUBLISHING
320 Broad Street
Red Bank, NJ 07701

First originally published by
Newman Springs Publishing 2021

ISBN 978-1-63692-534-9 (Paperback)
ISBN 978-1-63692-535-6 (Digital)

Printed in the United States of America

Of all the things in the world, nothing is
more beautiful to me than my girls.

Prologue

I stood staring out the window in the living room, watching the wind ripping through the leaves, with all the strength it could muster, tossing bits of branches to the ground. The night was all around me. Here I stood in our house, the house that was once filled with happiness and love, our little cottage. A place that made me feel safe and warm. Now it was dark, eerily so. Sad, empty, and lonely, and it was entirely my fault. I know that now; I guess I knew it all along, and I couldn't forgive myself. Would he be able to forgive me? I think not. I couldn't even begin to ask for his forgiveness. I didn't deserve it. I might not even want it.

This was the day I feared would come. The day that I had dreaded for months. If only I could have stopped myself. How could I have been so weak, so selfish? Now it was here. No getting away from it. How could I explain to a man who has loved me for so many years, a man who has given me such a good life? He was the man who held me in his arms for hours, with such love and devotion. He had always been truthful and loyal. I hated myself, and I wouldn't blame him if he hated me as well. I kept staring out the window, watching, looking down the dark, lonely road, waiting for his Mercedes to pull into the driveway, unsuspecting of what he was about to hear…

Chapter 1

I looked at myself in the trifold mirror above my dresser. I was wearing nothing but my new La Perla panty, simple black satin, which I had bought just for this very special occasion. I stared at my reflection in the mirror. I am not a beautiful woman. Pretty, yes, beautiful, no. I am not the kind of woman you would read about in a steamy romance novel. Nor do I belong on the cover of the *Sports Illustrated Swimsuit* issue. I have a fairly decent figure for a woman just about to turn forty. My breasts still stood at attention as if they had just heard the national anthem. My legs, while still looking good in a pair of shorts, do not go on for days. I cannot wrap them around my husband's back crisscross at the knees while we make love. Nice and Easy helped with the few strands of gray that decided to make their appearance on my shoulder-length chestnut-brown hair. I did, however, inherit my mother's beautiful, soft, unblemished skin.

I walked over to my closet and picked out something sexy, yet sophisticated, to wear for this special dinner. I couldn't believe it's our fifteenth anniversary. Where did the years go? I chose a simple black dress, high neck and no back. I knew that Jake will enjoy feeling the softness of my back as he slid his arm around my waist. It always gave me a soft tingle. I remembered as a young teenager my father saying, "Emma, if you are dressed from head to toe and you still get looks from the men, then you know you've got what it takes."

Funny, when I first met Jake, I was wearing blue jeans and a pale pink turtleneck. As odd as it may sound, I guess my father was right. I slipped on my dress and black pumps. I placed the two-carat diamond studs Jake had given me for our tenth anniversary in my ears. I put my hair up in a soft twist with just a few pins to hold it in place. I did this because I knew that Jake enjoyed removing them and watched my hair cascade around my shoulders when we would make love. Of course, this was where I hoped the evening would be heading. I so much enjoyed being with my husband. I looked in the mirror again; one last dab of my lipstick, and I'm done. Not bad for an almost forty-year-old. I grabbed my bag, and I was out the door.

I was to meet Jake at our favorite French restaurant in midtown at eight. He had one last appointment at his office and should be done by six. This would give him plenty of time to wrap up some paperwork and get to the restaurant. We decided to take an Uber instead of driving ourselves. We would both have a couple of drinks to celebrate our anniversary and didn't want to worry about driving home.

At seven forty-five, his cab arrived. I was standing in front of the restaurant watching him, as he paid the driver, and slid from the back seat. He looked so handsome in his dark-blue suit. It complimented his gray-blue eyes and silver-gray hair. I still couldn't believe that he was fifteen years my senior. Women still turn their heads to gaze at him. I never thought in my wildest dreams, what was I doing with someone so much older than me. He wasn't an old man. He was my husband, and I loved him very much.

He walked up to me, slid his arm around my waist, touching my bare skin, and gave me a gentle peck on the cheek. "You look great, Kid." He smiled. "Shall we eat?"

Kid was his term of endearment for me, since there was such a large gap in our ages. "Yes, please. I'm famished."

We walked into the lobby, hand in hand, and were greeted by Jill, our favorite hostess. "Dr. and Mrs. Farrell, how nice to see you again. Your table is ready."

She led us to the table in our favorite spot, quiet and cozy in a corner. A piano was playing the song "Someone to Watch over Me" in the background. Jake pulled out my chair, always the gentleman, and then he sat opposite me. He ordered our drinks, white wine for me, scotch rocks for him. He reached in his jacket pocket and whispered, "I have a little something for you, Kid. I hope you like it. I had it made especially for you."

I winked and whispered back, "Oh, Jake, you know it's not little." We both laughed at my off-color remark, and he smiled with pride as he placed a black velvet box on my bread plate. "Happy anniversary, Kid."

I opened the box, and there was a rose gold heart. My initials were encrusted with diamonds in the center. They sparkled so beautifully. I sprang from my chair. I walked around to where he was seated, bent down, and gave him a big kiss. "Oh, Jake, it's absolutely magnificent.

Who would have known that this beautiful heart could one day destroy a loving marriage?

He stood up and clasped the chain behind my neck. It fell perfectly on the front of my black dress. It looked stunning. He had such impeccable taste. We enjoyed our delicious meals. We sat quietly talking about our favorite memories of the past fifteen years, trying hard to avoid the sad ones. We went straight home after dinner and made love all night as I hoped we would. It was soft, gentle, passionate, and loving. He removed the pins from my hair and it fell softly around my shoulders. He slipped off my simple black dress and satin panty, but I left the beautiful heart around my neck. When we were done, there was my beautiful rose gold heart resting ever so gently between my breasts. I cuddled next to Jake, my head resting on his chest, listening to his heart beating. He had already drifted off and was fast asleep.

Chapter 2

I met Dr. James Richard Farrell, MD, or as I call him, "Jake," when I was just a mere girl of twenty-four. I had decided that I would go to the John Jay College of Criminal Justice for a masters in criminal psychology. I had always dreamt of someday working for the FBI's Behavioral Unit. I was very interested in the science of criminal profiling. I knew it would be a tremendous amount of work and studying and a long road ahead to get to that level in the FBI, but it was something I needed to try. The workings of the human mind had always intrigued me. What made people tic? What made certain people do the things they did and others the complete opposite? How could some people not care about the consequences of their actions while others stressed over killing a fly? Maybe, it was my obsession with forensics and law programs which I watched growing up, or the fact that my dad was a detective for the NYPD. Some of his cases fascinated me, although he was careful not to reveal too many gruesome details. We loved to watch detective shows together. Dad would often comment that these shows were not exactly accurate. Theatrics, you know, real Hollywood. He would beam with pride when he would tell me how many cases he solved.

And so on one chilly October morning, I slipped on my jeans and pale pink turtleneck sweater. I rushed over to John Jay to hear a guest speaker lecture on "Abnormal Psychology and Modern Life." The sub-topic being anxiety disorders, particularly post-traumatic stress disorders, and acute stress disorders with delayed onsets. Anything I could learn would greatly help. When I walked into the conference center, I took a seat in the front of the room. There were not too many seats left. The room was filled to capacity. Jake walked in from the side entrance of the room and stood at the podium. When he began speaking, there was complete silence. Everyone listened so intently to his every word. Students scribbled down notes and some typed on their laptops. He was brilliant, assured, articulate, and well, truth be said, sexy in the older teacher sort of way. The kind you flipped over in your freshman year of high school. You couldn't wait to get to his class and then wondered why you would barely pass. Could it be because you dreamt of marrying him and were not listening to a single word he said? I took notes, listened carefully, and hoped I could get a quick word with him at the end of the lecture.

When he was finished speaking, I was totally disappointed. First, I found the lecture extremely interesting and didn't want it to end. He asked if anyone had questions, and a number of hands went up. He answered each one in great detail. Secondly, I enjoyed watching and listening to Jake.

He was, I don't know…HOT. Maybe I could fake some kind of stress disorder and make an appointment at Dr. Farrell's office…just kidding.

I did, however, have to say something before he left. I walked up to the podium where other students were telling him how much they enjoyed his lecture. I really just wanted to say "I enjoyed you," but I just shook his hand and blurted, "I think you were great, Dr. Farrell."

Oh my god, did I just say that? I felt like such a nerd.

He smiled. "Thank you, that's very kind. And your name is?"

"Emma, Emma Flynn."

We spoke a little longer about the lecture and my interest in criminal psychology. I asked a few questions, and he answered each one. Then he suddenly looked at his watch. *I think I must be boring him or he has someplace else to be. Either way, this conversation was over.* I felt my heart sink.

"Emma, I have about an hour before my first appointment of the day, would you like to continue this conversation over a cup of coffee, tea, latte, your choice?"

Was this really happening? Oh god. I nodded in the affirmative, too stunned to speak. We walked to a nearby Starbucks. I chose a grande macchiato. Oddly enough, I didn't even remember drinking it. I was too engrossed in Jake. And so our relationship began.

We started off slow. It was more like a teacher-taking-a-student-under-his-wing than a date. We visited MoMA, the Museum of Natural History, went to the theater, and he was always the quintessential gentleman. He made me feel like I had his full, undivided attention and my interests were very important to him. We would sit on benches in Central Park and talk about psychology, forensics, and his work cases. He was careful not to divulge any names. Doctor/patient confidentiality, you know.

I would ramble on and on about my interest in the behavioral sciences, and he would listen to my every word. Jake didn't talk too much about his background, but obviously, he was very successful in life. He never mentioned anything about ever being married, having a girlfriend, or having children from previous relationships. His biography online said he was single. *Yay!*

We talked about my life and family. Especially, my NYPD-blue detective dad. He wasn't too keen on the idea of my dating a man fifteen years my senior. I never mentioned this to Jake. I hoped it would pass when and if he met him. I told Jake how I had lost my mom. She was killed by a hit-and-run. They never caught the driver. This destroyed my dad. His being on the police force and not being able to catch the person who killed my mom just crossing the street. And so my father turned all his love and attention to me. He was both mom and dad. He was super protective, trying to do his best to give me a good life. I loved and respected him for that. Maybe, Jake could meet Dad at Christmastime. The festive season might soften Dad up a bit.

We made love for the first time the week before Christmas. We had a quick dinner at a restaurant in midtown and decided to walk over to see the Christmas tree at Rockefeller Center. The weather was cold and windy, and we huddled together as we walked through the crowds. The city was decorated in all its Christmas finery. It began to flurry, which gave the city a special Christmas glow. I loved this time of year. This year would be especially merry; I could feel it. We looked at the tree for a few minutes. I turned to look up at Jake. I was just about to say how much I was enjoying the evening when he looked down and smiled at me.

"Come home with me tonight, Kid."

The words I had hoped to hear for three months had finally been spoken. I leaned into his chest and whispered, "I would love to." My heart was pounding so loudly I thought he might hear it. He took me by the hand and led me through the Christmas crowds.

On the way to his condo in River Towers, my mind raced. I prayed that I would not disappoint him, in any way. I wasn't experienced in the love-making department. I had only one experience with a sexual encounter, and that didn't go very well. I was too young, scared, and not really in love—a recipe for a complete disaster. Surely, a man of his success, charm, and sex appeal would have had many women. Yet, I had a feeling he would guide me through.

It was magical. He was amazing. It was as if he could read my mind and sensed my lack of experience. He was gentle and patient. It was as if he was teaching me how to use my body and give it to him, which I did, with my whole heart. He would be the teacher, and I his willing pupil. He read my body as if it was on the *New York Times* best seller list. This would be a very Merry Christmas on many levels.

When he was asleep, I slipped out of the bed and explored the apartment. It was very much a man's apartment. Dark colors. Bare, not much in the way of decorations. No hint of a woman's touch. Good. One thing that caught my eye was the view from the living-room window on the west side of the apartment. From the fifteenth floor, the view was amazing. Below, in the river, there was the aircraft carrier, the Intrepid. It was very impressive. I was so engrossed in the view, I didn't hear Jake sneak up behind me. "Jake, this is amazing."

"I like this view too," he whispered. "It's something that has always made me feel especially patriotic."

I leaned back against his chest. "It must be wonderful to look out your window every day and have such a magnificent sight. You're very lucky."

"Yes, I guess I am, Emma." He kissed the back of my head, and I knew he wasn't just talking about the view.

He looked down at the aircraft carrier and surprisingly started to speak about his brother. Something he had never done before. "My brother, Dean, was in the military, and I have a tremendous amount of respect for our men and women who sacrifice everything for us."

As he said this, I thought I saw a tear swell in his beautiful sleepy blue eyes. He stopped talking. I turned and kissed his chest. He led me back into the bedroom. We made love again. This time, I was more relaxed and a little more self-assured. I fell asleep in his arms, and I knew that's where I would still be in the morning.

When I awoke, there was a note on the black marble kitchen island telling me that he had an early appointment and he would call me later. I was on Christmas break, so there was no need for me to rush out. I took a long, soothing shower. I let the hot water run over my very much newly alive body. The bathroom had the fresh and clean scent from Jake's previous shower. *God, I love that scent.* I made myself a cup of coffee and dressed. I caught the train home to Brooklyn Heights.

When I arrived home, Dad was waiting in the kitchen, drinking a cup of coffee and looking very concerned. "Are you sure you know what you're doing, sweetheart? He is a lot older."

I gave him a quick hug. He always has my best interest at heart. "I know what I'm doing, Detective. Trust me, please."

That was the end of the conversation…for now.

Chapter 3

Six weeks had passed since our very Merry Christmas. Our relationship was growing very nicely. I had extremely strong feelings for Jake. I was hoping that he felt the same way about me. He seemed to, but the words were never spoken. Even after we made love, I wanted to tell him how I felt. I wanted to say "I think I am falling in love with you" but I didn't. I would be devastated if he didn't reciprocate the feelings. So I would just lie quietly in his arms.

My father was getting used to the fact that I was spending more and more time at Jake's apartment. I thought it would be a good idea if I called and asked him if he would like to have a quiet dinner and spend some quality time with his favorite daughter. We could just relax and watch some of our old favorite detective shows, on his new big-screen TV. He would often boast, "I can do a better job than that." And I would laugh. I didn't want him to feel like I was neglecting my favorite father. I was spending so much time with Jake, it was the least I could do.

We ordered Chinese takeout, sat on the couch, and turned on some *Law and Order* reruns. Midway through my lo mein, I started to feel quite sick to my stomach. I ran in the bathroom, closed the door behind me, and began vomiting. My father followed me, knocked on the door, and asked if I was all right.

"It must be some bad lo mein, Dad. I'll be fine in a minute."

I sat on the floor and waited for my stomach to settle. When it didn't, I opened the door and told Dad, who was looking a little pale with worry himself, that I felt a bit better but decided to turn in for the night. I would feel much better in the morning, I hoped. I slipped into my bed and pulled the covers up over my head. After a couple of hours of lying in misery, I finally fell asleep. When I awoke around six thirty, I headed straight for the bathroom. *This was not good. Not good at all.* I crawled back into bed and pretended to be asleep. I didn't want my father to see me in this condition. I stayed under the covers until he left for work. He poked his head in to check on me and then left. I rolled over and lay on my back, staring at the ceiling.

Can it be morning sickness? I could feel the panic growing. Was I just overreacting? Was my mind running away with itself? *Maybe it really was bad lo mein. Could I be that lucky?* I decided to wait a week to see how I felt. I hadn't even realized my period should have started a week ago. With any luck, this sick feeling would pass. During the following week, I imagined every possible scenario. Maybe I was sick or just rundown. I would come home from class and lie on the couch, tears running down my face. I could barely make it through my classes. Once again, I would find myself in the bathroom on the floor. All that week, I tried my best to avoid seeing or speaking to Jake. I made one excuse after another. I was working on papers for class. I had a massive headache, or Dad isn't feeling well. *Hell was freezing over.* Dad's detective instincts were starting to get suspicious. I could tell, but he said nothing.

On Saturday, I went over to the pharmacy and bought a home pregnancy test. I went into the bathroom, locked the door, and followed the directions. When, there on the stick, a pretty little YES appeared. My whole body started to shake.

How could this have happened? Oh, I know how it happened, but how can I be pregnant? We were always so careful, except for that first night before Christmas.

Jake must have assumed that a twenty-four-year-old would have known how to take care of these things. He must have thought I was on the pill. I was so anxious and excited that night that I didn't even think to ask about condoms. I was so much into being with Jake; protection was the furthest thing from my mind. Now I felt like a stupid sixteen-year-old who was fumbling in the back seat of her boyfriend's car. I sat on the couch and cried, thinking of every way I might handle this very upsetting situation.

Abortion, oh god no, I could never. Should I keep the child and raise it on my own? How would Jake react to having a son or daughter and not being in the child's life? Don't tell Jake, move away, and he'll never know. Give it up for adoption, no. What do I do about my dream of working for the behavioral unit? How do I handle both?

My mind was spinning. I was sick, sick to my stomach. I didn't budge all day. Then it dawned on me. *Honesty*—tell Jake the truth. See his reaction and accept it, whatever it might be. However hard it might be, listen to what he had to say. I heard the door open behind me; my father was coming home from work. I won't say anything to my father just yet; he still carried a gun. I must get Jake's reaction first.

I called his office and asked the receptionist if I could have a quick word with him. She told me that he was in with a patient, but she would give him the message and have him call me back. I think she had a little bit of a crush on him. And why not? He was something special, especially to me. I waited for-ty-five minutes before my cell rang. My hands started to tremble as I answered.

"Emma, how are you feeling?"

I was not surprised at the question, since I had every disease under the sun this week just to avoid seeing him. I said fine. *Liar.* I could not tell him my overwhelming news on the phone, so I asked if he could meet me at the Starbucks by his office. I could hear in his voice that he sensed something was wrong. We decided on eight. He had to finish out his appointments. This would give me a chance to shower, dress, and make myself look more present-able. I hoped some eye makeup would camouflage the red puffy eyes. I walked out the door in a fog. This could either go very well or horrifically wrong. I would know the answer in just an hour.

When I arrived, at Starbucks, Jake hadn't arrived yet. The waiting was killing me. He walked through the door at eight ten. Those ten minutes felt like ten years. I didn't know if I felt like vomiting from nerves or the pregnancy. He had a concerned look on his face and gave me a big hug.

"I missed you, Emma. What's going on?"

I took a deep breath. I could feel a lump swelling in my throat. I had to fight back the tears. How do I start? *Oh, Jake I am about to ruin your life.* Yes, that's it. I'll tell him that. I'm sure he'll be delighted. No. He had to see me strong, not scared of his reaction, but confident in what I was about to say. I looked into his concerned blue eyes.

"Jake, I'm going to have a baby." There I said it.

He just stared at me for what seemed forever but was just a moment. I didn't think he was sure of what he had just heard. Then, as if magical, a smile grew across his face. "Well, it's about time. My biological clock is ticking, Emma. I'm almost forty, you know. I always wanted to be a dad." He reached for my hand.

"Jake, don't joke. This is serious. It will change both our lives forever."

He slowly took the palm of his other hand and placed it on my lower abdomen. "Thank you, Kid. I know this is a shock, a very big shock, but it is something I knew I would want someday. Now you have given it to me. That someday is now. I love you, and I will love this child. There is only one problem."

Here it comes, I thought. *I knew it.*

"I will have to cancel my schedule for the next month so we can have a nice wedding and a beautiful romantic honeymoon."

Oh my god, the man wanted to marry me. Of course I said yes. This was not the reaction I was expecting, not at all.

We had a small ceremony. I didn't want a big fancy wedding. I was still in shock that Jake was happy about the pregnancy. We had a quiet ceremony in church. I wore a simple white suit and my mother's pearl necklace. After the ceremony, we went to dinner with a few close family and friends. My dad, surprisingly enough, was being the proud future grandpa. He was taking this all rather well. Jake and I went home and made love like honeymooners. He was being so careful. I think he thought that I would break.

"Jake, I don't think the baby knows what's going on. I think you can go for it, Daddy."

His passion grew with the thought that he had created a life, and it was like we were making love for the first time again. Actually, we were making love for the first time as Mr. and Mrs. Farrell.

"Did I shock the baby?" he said with pride in his voice.

"No, Jake, just me." I laughed. I didn't realize being pregnant heightened the intensity of my arousal, but did it ever.

He looked into my eyes, slid down my body with his lips, and kissed my stomach. "Thank you again, Mrs. Farrell." He rested his ear on my stomach as if he was listening for the baby.

"You are most welcome, Mr. Farrell."

He gave me a deep, passionate kiss, rolled over, and fell asleep.

We took a small honeymoon in the Hamptons. It was so beautiful. Jake wanted to take me on an extensive European vacation. I was definitely not feeling up to it. I didn't think the traveling would help my morning sickness. So we drove to the Hamptons, and it was just the honeymoon I needed. There were Jake and I and the little peanut resting ever so happily in my belly. It was a relaxing and quiet vacation. We rented a small country cottage. It was just perfect. It was not the summer season, so restaurants and shops were all pretty much empty. There was no rush of the crowds that the summer months would bring. Jake promised to buy me a home in the Hamptons one day because I loved it so much. I knew he would keep his word.

Time passed, and I was due for my fourth month OB/GYN checkup with Dr. DiMario this coming Friday. I was so excited. Jake had decided to cut his appointments short that day and come with me. It would be the first time he would hear little peanut's heartbeat. I had heard it on the previous checkups. It was an amazing sound. I couldn't wait for Jake to hear it as well. We arrived at the doctor's office around three. Dr. DiMario was just finishing up with a couple.

Their baby was due any day. She looked like she would explode. I looked down at my little baby bump and whispered to Jake, "Can you believe I will look like that in a few months?"

He smiled, put his hand on my bump, and said, "You mean beautiful? You already do." He always knew just the right thing to say.

The sonogram technician called us in. Jake sat on the stool in the corner of the room. I slipped on my gown and climbed onto the table. "Please, lay back, Mrs. Farrell. This will feel a little cold for a second." She squeezed a pink jelly on my stomach and started to move the monitor back and forth. We could see the baby, but there was no movement or a heartbeat. She checked the machine's volume and tried again.

"Oh, he's being a bit difficult today, little bugger. No need to worry, Mrs. Farrell. Just let me bring in Dr. DiMario to recheck." She walked out of the room.

Jake stood up and held my hand. I could feel my heart drop. I could see the worried look on Jake's face.

Dr. DiMario came into the room. He had a guarded smile on his face. "Okay, Emma, let's have a look here." He repeated the test, which had the same results.

Tears began streaming down my cheeks. Jake's eyes started to flood.

"I am so sorry, Emma. There is no heartbeat." He held my hand and gave me a sad smile. "These things happen. I can't be sure why. It's not anything you've done or didn't do."

He put his hand on Jake's shoulder. "I'll give you two some alone time. Again, I am so very sorry." He stepped out of the room.

Jake bent down and kissed my forehead, tears running down his face. I could see the baby on the monitor. I wanted to yell, "*Wake up, move*, please move." The little peanut was gone. But how could that be? He was right there in my growing belly resting quietly.

"Jake, why? Please, help me to understand why these things happen."

He had no answers, only tears. I was brought to the hospital and given medication to bring on labor. A day later, I lost my little peanut.

We tried two more times after we lost our first baby. Each time, I would barely make it through my first trimester when my doctor's visit would inexplicably take a turn for the worst. I began dreading the doctor's appointments and the excitement that came with a positive pregnancy test. One night, huddled in bed after my third miscarriage, we decided that the hurt was becoming too unbearable for both of us. There wouldn't be another time around. We would just go on together and find happiness in each other; that's all that was important. That's all that we needed. I did so much want to be a mother, but it seemed that it wasn't meant for me. Adoption was an option, but I couldn't think about that right now. I remember that moment in bed, as clear as day, Jake kissing my temple and saying, "I love you no matter what. It's you and me, Kid."

And so that's how it went. Jake had his growing practice. And me, well, I decided to stop classes for my masters. As much as I loved forensics, my head wasn't ready to deal with all the work and study. It might have been a distraction, but I didn't feel that way at the time. I decided, with Jake's blessings, to stay home for a while. I volunteered at the local library. I would do storytime with preschoolers and teach them arts and crafts. I do love children, and wanted to be around them in some way. I found it rewarding, and the children were such fun. Staying home for a while turned into the passing years.

All seemed to be going well…and it did for the next fifteen years.

Chapter 4

    Jake's practice was going extremely well and had grown quite considerably. So it was no surprise when he received a phone call from the Veteran's Health Care System. They had asked Jake if he would be interested in working with veterans who had come home from overseas and were suffering from post-traumatic stress disorder. Since this was one of his fields of expertise, I knew he would definitely consider it. He had called me at home and asked me to meet him for lunch. He wanted to discuss my thoughts on his undertaking such a task. He knew that this meant a lot of long hours at the office and time away from home.

    I thought back to shortly after we were married. I was looking out my favorite window, down at the Intrepid. I did love that beautiful view. I remembered Jake's sad face when he spoke about his brother that first night we spent together. I was curious as to why he never mentioned him again or never asked his brother to meet me. I just assumed they were not a close family. I was sure he had his reasons, so I just did not press the issue. Why did Jake appear so sad when he looked down at the Intrepid? I summoned my courage at last and asked Jake about his brother's tour in the military. I hoped he would open up to me. He did.

Dean had served in the Gulf War. When Dean came home from overseas, he was not himself anymore. He suffered from nightmares, anxiety, and guilt. He suffered trauma from things he had done, things he had seen, and things he had been ordered to do. He began drinking heavily, and on one rainy night, he drove his car off a back road on Long Island. The car flipped over, and Dean, who had been too drunk to even think about a seat belt, went through the wind shield and was killed instantly. I hadn't imagined the tears I thought I saw in Jake's eyes. He had tried to help Dean, talking, taking him in, but to no avail. Now this would be his second chance to make up for how he thought he had failed his brother. If he couldn't help his brother, maybe he could help someone else's brother, son, daughter, sister, husband, or wife. He was going to ask me my thoughts on the matter. What could I possible say?

How could I tell him it would be too much for him to handle when I knew this was something he needed to do? It could bring back so many upsetting memories of Dean, memories he might have chosen to forget. However, his heart and mind were telling him he needed to do this for his brother.

At lunch, he explained to me the work he would be undertaking. I listened carefully. He was so intent on explaining how much this meant to him. I could tell he wanted to do this so badly. He would have conferences with other doctors at the Veteran's Health Care System. In the weeks ahead, he would discuss the programs they would be implementing and how many patients he would have on his schedule. I knew his mind was made up. I smiled and gave him my blessing.

For the next few weeks, he worked day and night. He met with other psychiatrists to review and study a number of case files. He did research on the veterans he would have as his patients. I could see the dedication to his work and on his face. I knew he would give it his all. He had to do this for Dean and for himself. I kept busy with my work at the library, which I was still doing and enjoying. I also worked for a number of charities, many of which involved children's illnesses. I did this for the little peanut I lost so many years ago but still carried in my heart.

Jake and I hardly saw each other those first few weeks, but it was for a very good cause. These men and women had served their country and deserved all the help and respect we could give. The time was growing near for Jake to start seeing his patients. He was very excited but nervous as well. What if he couldn't help them? Their mental well-being was in his hands. He wanted so desperately to make a difference. I knew he would do it. He wouldn't let himself fail.

His first appointment was scheduled for Friday afternoon at four. He told me that the appointment would be about an hour, but given the fact that it was the first time he would be meeting with this Marine, it might take a little longer. He didn't want to rush him out of the office. He wanted to give him his undivided attention, especially on his first visit. He was suffering from PTSD and was one of the more serious cases. He was pretty much alone, from what Jake had read in his case files, and desperately needed someone to talk to.

Jake suggested that I meet him for dinner after his last appointment. Something we hadn't done in weeks. We needed some alone time, and I was also anxious to hear how the appointment had gone. I knew he wouldn't be able to give me great details or names. Still, I was very curious.

I would be able to tell by his demeanor during dinner. If he felt it went well, there would be such excitement in his voice as he spoke about the session. If not, I would be supportive and reassure him that he could only do his best. He knew that it would take time for his patients to totally open up to him. Some don't even want to talk about their tours. They simply want to forget. These vets would need a lot of help. Many of their scars were not just on their bodies but deeply rooted mentally. They needed time to let their emotions come to the surface.

It was six thirty when I rushed into the Medical Arts building where Jake had his office. I was running late. Traffic in the city was a nightmare as usual. I hurried to the elevators in the gray marble lobby. When the elevator doors opened, I slammed right into a young man coming out of the elevator. I was not watching where I was going and stumbled. He reached out and grabbed me around the waist. I apologized profusely, but when I looked up, I was stunned at this amazingly handsome face standing in front of me. He held me around my waist.

"No problem. The way my day has been going, this is the best thing that's happened to me all day." He laughed and flashed a beautiful smile, one little crooked tooth on the bottom, his only imperfection.

He was tall, at least a head over me, wavy dark-brown hair combed back, and he had the most piercing blue eyes I had ever seen. His jaw was chiseled with a clef in his chin, covered slightly by a faint five o'clock shadow. I knew I was staring, but I couldn't turn away. What was wrong with me? His scent was intoxicating; I wondered which cologne he was wearing? A scar went through his left eyebrow, which only made his face all the more intriguing and added to his sex appeal. He wore a pair of blue jeans and a khaki T-shirt. This showed off his flat stomach and the strong muscles of his arms and chest. He was a perfect specimen of a man. He was a real man's man. He was a real woman's man for that matter. I had all to do to stop staring at him. Yet, there was something solemn about him. Why would someone so perfect look so lost?

I apologized again. He stepped aside with a grin and watched as I entered the elevator. As the doors closed, I felt a warm flush come over me. It felt so strange. How can a simple bump into a stranger leave my heart pounding in my chest? Something about this man had my head spinning and my heart pounding. As I got to Jake's office, he was just locking the door. I still felt flushed. His receptionist had already gone for the day, so it was just Jake and I.

"Shall we go, Kid? I'm starved."

I just gave him a bright smile and took his arm. I was feeling a little guilty about my reaction to the stranger, but it was just a harmless bump.

We were off to our restaurant. All through dinner, Jake spoke about how grateful he was for the opportunity to be helping these servicemen and women. So I assumed it went well.

During dinner, I could not help but think about the stranger coming out of the elevator. His eyes, his body, and the smell of the cologne he was wearing. Why did he have such an effect on my mind and body? I've seen many a handsome man in my day, but this was different. I just couldn't get him out of my mind. Was it the lost look in his eyes? He was the type of man when you roll over in the morning and see him lying naked next to you in bed, you think to yourself…boy, I did good last night.

That night, after dinner, Jake and I went straight home and made love, or what I would call intense sex, which I initiated. Jake was more than willing to oblige. I helped Jake out of his clothes and quickly slipped off mine.

"Slow down, Kid. What's the rush?"

I kept seeing that amazing face. My body made love to Jake, but my mind was on the stranger in the elevator. I would close my eyes and see those amazing, magnetic blue eyes staring down at me as if I were making love to him. Every time I thought about that face, the height of my arousal was beyond words. When we were done, Jake looked at me quite surprised. Our sex life was always warm, passionate and intimate, but this was totally different.

"What brought that on? You were amazing, Kid."

Not that he was complaining.

"I missed you these past few weeks. You've been so busy. I just needed to be with you."

I lied. I did need to be with Jake. I wanted to be with Jake, but it was the man coming out of the elevator that my mind and body were responding to. I hoped I would run into that face again.

I felt terribly guilty. But it was just a harmless fantasy…right?

The following week, the man from the elevator continually raced through my thoughts. *I just couldn't forget him. I must be going through a midlife crisis. After all, almost turning forty would do that to a woman.* I just couldn't stop thinking about the lovemaking with Jake after I had seen the stranger in the elevator. It was unbelievable. How it had affected my pleasure. I was all over Jake that next week, and he loved it. Every time I thought of the stranger during sex, it got more intense. I had to see that face again. I wondered who he was, and if he was married…lucky girl. What was he doing in Jake's building? Mostly, I wondered how he was in bed. Was he gentle? Was he passionate? Just lying next to him and touching that body and face would bring me to the brink. That's all I would need. I thought of ways I could run into him again.

I also thought, Emma, stop this, you're acting like a sixteen-year-old cheerleader obsessed with the star quarterback.

I would laugh and think that I wouldn't mind scoring a touchdown with him. I did feel somewhat guilty, but what harm was there in a little fantasy? I'm sure all women did it. It would not be normal not to fantasize. It's only human nature. *It was harmless, really.*

I kept hoping I would see him again someday. Impossible. There are millions of people in the city, what would be the odds. Then I had a thought… I ran into him leaving Jake's building. Maybe, he worked there, or did he see a doctor in the building? There were a number of offices in that building. He might need to go there again. Not that I hoped he was ill, but after all, it was a medical arts building. I would go and wait outside, same time, six thirty, same day, Friday. If Jake should happen to come out of the building, I could say I was on my way to surprise him for dinner.

My god, I feel like such a bitch, but I only want to see that face. It's not like I'm betraying Jake. He didn't deserve that, not at all. I just wanted to see the man from the elevator one more time. He probably wouldn't even be there. I was just having some fun. It was completely innocent. Harmless, really.

Chapter 5

I woke up Friday morning, anxious for the plot that was unfolding in my mind. I didn't have the library today, so I thought I would do something to keep myself busy. If I didn't, I would stress myself to the max. I decided to take a trip over to the Macy's on Thirty-Fourth Street. I threw on some leggings and a tee. I put my hair in a ponytail, and off I went. I could use some new makeup, maybe a Dior or Chanel lipstick. A new perfume would be nice, too, something light and airy.

I walked into Macy's main floor, passed the handbags, and went into the cosmetics and fragrance department. The scent of the perfumes and colognes filled the air. As I walked to the Chanel counter, a gentleman in a black shirt and slacks approached me with a little white card. I knew what that meant. He wanted me to smell the scent sprayed on the card.

"Buying new cologne for the man in your life?" He laughed.

At first, I said no, but the smell seemed oddly familiar. I took a sniff of the small rectangular card.

It was the cologne Mr. Elevator was wearing. Who could forget that scent? I asked the gentleman which cologne it was, and he directed me to the counter and showed me the bottle. I sprayed a small amount of the cologne on my wrist and took a deep breath. My head started to spin; this was it. That scent would drive me crazy. I told the salesman I would have to think about it. I said that my husband was very particular about which colognes he wore, but *I* certainly loved it. I went to the cosmetics counter and decided on a nice rose color lipstick from Chanel.

I didn't go to the perfume counters. I didn't want them to interfere with the scent on my wrist. I walked around Macy's for an hour or so. The whole time sniffing my wrist and daydreaming. When I got home, I thought that I must be losing my mind. It was a good thing I was married to an excellent psychiatrist. I could just hear my therapy session with him.

"Well, Jake, I'm obsessed with a man I bumped into as he was getting off the elevator in your building last week, when I was rushing to meet you for dinner on Friday. I sprayed his cologne, or what I think was his cologne, on my wrist while I was in Macy's shopping for a new lipstick. I walked around sniffing the cologne on my arm all day, just to imagine his scent. I'm planning on stalking him if he leaves your office building just to get another glimpse of him. The best part is when we have sex, I picture his face looking down at me and his body on top of mine in bed. It drives me wild."

Yep, that should go over really big. Next stop, divorce court and a new psychiatrist.

I'm sorry, Jake, I kept telling myself over and over in my head. But I couldn't help myself. It was fun and exciting, doing something daring. Something I would have never thought of doing in the past. I turned on the TV and watched some cooking show—not that I was a huge fan of cooking, but it was something to pass the time. I'll start getting ready for my adventure around four. I picked out a pair of jeans, a white tank top, and a red blazer. I took a shower, blew my hair, put on my new lipstick, and my usual perfume. When I was dressed, I went to my jewelry box and put on my rose-gold-and-diamond initial necklace. If I ran into Jake, I wanted him to see me wearing it. The diamonds in the E and F shone so brightly. It truly was a beautiful piece. Jake had always been so generous with his gifts. I looked at my watch; it was time to go.

I headed to Jake's office building. My heart was pounding. I couldn't believe I was really doing this. I arrived at the building around six thirty, right around the time I had seen him leaving the last time. If Mr. Elevator comes out of the building, I would get another glimpse of him. I'll call Jake on his cell and tell him that I was going into Brooklyn to see my dad. This way I could follow him for a while, just to see where he goes. If Mr. Elevator doesn't come out of the building, I'll call Jake and say that I was downstairs. I wanted to surprise him for dinner. He should be almost done with his patients by now.

Oh my god. Doesn't that make me sound so deceitful?

While I was waiting outside the building, I noticed a young man in a camouflage jacket, missing one leg sitting on the sidewalk holding a plastic cup, and a small dog lying by his side. They both desperately needed a bath and a good meal. Some people dropped money in the cup as they passed, others just walked by. I started to think. Jake had told me that he had a number of patients who had really seen horrifying acts against humanity on their tours overseas. They saw deaths of innocent women and children. Fellow marines and friends had been blown up in bombings. Many had lost limbs. Some had battle scars on their bodies. A number of them had mental scars that would take a long time to heal, if they would ever truly heal at all.

Jake was trying his best to help these poor, unfortunate souls come back to some kind of normal life. I think the hardest part for these returning soldiers was the fact that while many people respected them and thanked them for their service, a number of people just didn't seem to care. People seeing them sleeping on park benches, begging on roadway off ramps, or sitting on curbs were becoming all too commonplace for many. These soldiers were left homeless. These men fought for our country. They protected us. Where were their rights to a good life?

Jake wanted to be a part of the people who said thank you, in his own way, be it professional or just respectful. He spent many nights researching his cases. He was a good man and doctor, why was I doing such a foolish thing to such a decent man? Just for a bit of harmless fun. I just couldn't do this. I decided to go home. I felt ridiculous and foolish. Why would I lie to Jake if he walked out of the building? I just couldn't do it. I started to walk toward the corner to hail a cab. I wanted to get home before Jake and start some form of dinner. Then suddenly, I felt someone tap me on the shoulder.

"Excuse me, miss, aren't you the crazy lady who bumps into people getting off elevators?"

I turned, and there he was. If I willed this to happen, it wouldn't in a million years. What were the odds?

I composed myself. "Oh yes, that was me, crazy elevator lady. I make it a habit of running into perfect strangers getting off elevators, just for the fun of it. I like to see how many people I could knock down." I smiled. *I really did mean perfect.* He was totally perfect.

A number of cabs passed, but I hailed none. They were a sea of yellow vehicles all moving in the same direction right now. Crowds of people started to cross the street. I just stood there. *What do I do now? Should I continue to talk to him? Apologize once more for the other day? Should I say have a good evening and just walk away? I thought, God, he is gorgeous. Boy, the things I would want to do to him can only be described as pornographic. My mind and heart kept saying, Emma, go home, you're being ridiculous. My body kept saying, Emma, find the nearest motel and go for it.*

He looked down at my rose-gold heart. "E. F., what does that stand for?"

I forgot about the heart around my neck. I couldn't tell him my correct name. So I did the next best thing, I lied.

"Elizabeth Flynn." Well, it wasn't a total lie, really, Flynn was my maiden's name. "And you are? Oh, wait, I know, Mr. Elevator Man." We both laughed.

"Well, Elizabeth, how would you like to join Mr. Elevator Man for a drink?" He noticed my wedding band, but it didn't seem to matter much to him.

"Thank you really, but I can't. I have to meet my husband for dinner." Again, the word *husband* didn't seem to be an issue for him. Maybe, it was just an innocent friendly drink he was offering, and I was reading too much into it. I was too frazzled because of what was going through my mind. I didn't answer.

"Well, I guess not, maybe another time." He turned and started to walk away.

Another time, when would there possibly be another time? I had to say something.

"Well, maybe, just a very quick one. After all, I did almost kill you by the elevator. Tell you what, my treat. I do have at least an hour before I meet my husband."

Another lie. Emma, what are you doing? He turned back and gave me a big smile.

We walked a block or two and stopped at a small bistro. The place was crowded with people having drinks after work. We found a seat and sat at the bar.

I ordered my usual white wine. He ordered a Jack Daniel's. We made small talk. I told him about my work in the library and that my father was a retired NYPD detective. I always thought it was a good idea to let a stranger know that I was related to a man who carried a gun. He obviously knew I was married, but I didn't say anything about Jake or what he did for a living nor did he ask. He told me he was originally from Pennsylvania but was now living in Alphabet City in Manhattan. I didn't offer where I lived. I just loved looking at him, talking, and sitting with him at the bar. About twenty minutes into the conversation, my cell went off.

It was Jake. I excused myself and said I needed to take the call, it was my husband checking on our dinner plans. I walked to the back of the bar. In fact, it was Jake calling to tell me he needed to finish some paperwork and put some information in his computer. He would be home late and not to wait up for him. I told him that it was fine and this would give me a chance to go into Brooklyn and visit with my dad for a few hours. I certainly wasn't going to tell him I was sitting in a bar with a man I have been fantasizing about for the past week. Jake suggested that I spend the night. *Now that's an idea. Just kidding.* He didn't want me coming home late by myself. He would see me first thing in the morning. I told him I loved him. I really do.

"I love you too, Kid." And he hung up.

As I turned, I noticed my new friend was standing behind me, listening to my every word.

"Sounds like you have a free night, or are you really going to visit your dad?" I was stunned that he had followed me to the back of the bar and was listening to me every word.

I shook my head no. He bent down and gave me a slow, gentle kiss. I pushed him away, both hands on his chest, but he didn't budge. He slipped his hand around my waist and pulled me closer to him. Again, he kissed me. This time, the kiss was more heated. I could feel the strength of his arm around my waist. The hardness of his muscular chest pressing against my own breast made my heart race. I looked up at those blue eyes. This time, I didn't resist. I kissed him back. His kisses were slow and methodical. I found myself leaning against the wall to hold myself up. My legs were getting weak. I could feel my body starting to respond to his body against mine. I put my arms around him; I could feel the strong muscles of his back.

"I don't even know your name," I murmured. Not that it mattered at that point.

"Ethan," he whispered in my ear.

Chapter 6

We walked out of the bistro. My head spinning from the wine and his amazing kisses. He went to the curb and hailed a cab. He helped me in the car and slid next to me. *I shouldn't be doing this. I'm taking such a risk at ruining what is a good marriage.* This was getting beyond harmless, and yet I couldn't stop myself. How could I let myself get in a cab with a perfect stranger? I thought that he would get in the cab and start kissing me again. I waited. But he didn't. He gave the driver an address somewhere in Alphabet City, but I barely heard it. He didn't say a word, he didn't make a move. It was as if he was making me wait for what I knew would eventually happen. I could feel my heart pounding. I was aching for him, just looking at that handsome face, breathing in that mind-blowing cologne, and sitting next to that magnificent body. I would have made love to him, right here in the back seat of the cab if it weren't for rearview mirrors. Why was I taking such a crazy chance?

The cab pulled up to a red brick building, with a small stoop. A brown fire escape came down from the fifth floor in front of the building. He held my hand and led me up the front steps. He slipped his key in the front door, and we were in a small foyer. I could smell a coat of fresh paint. It had a small black-and-white tile floor. He unlocked the second door, and we started to climb the stairs. On the second landing, he opened the door to his studio apartment. It was barely furnished. There was a small kitchen with a table and two chairs.

IKEA, I would guess. There was a couch facing a large-screen television in the corner of the room. Behind the couch was a queen size bed with a nightstand and lamp. The bed was neatly made. The bathroom was to the left of the bed. I asked if I could use the bathroom, and of course, he said yes. I walked in and rested my head against the bathroom door, hardly able to breathe. I went to the sink and splashed cool water on my face. *What do I do next?* This was not me, but I wanted him so badly. It wasn't love, obviously. I didn't even know this man. It was lust, definitely lust, pure and simple. It was the desire to hold that body and to kiss that amazing face.

I took off my blazer and stepped out of the bathroom. He had removed his shirt, shoes, and socks and was sitting on the couch waiting for me. He stood up and started walking toward me, looking into my eyes the whole time. The sun was setting, and the apartment was getting dimly lit with a golden glow. As I got closer to him, I could see a tattoo across his left pectoral. It read "*Semper Fi.*"

Oh my god, he's a marine. A marine coming out of Jake's building. Was he one of Jake's patients? What were the odds of that happening? It can't be. I could see a scar coming around from the left side of his back around to his stomach. It must have been a terrible wound. *I thought to myself again, could he be one of my husband's patients? No, impossible.* He took my hand and led me over to the bed. I pulled my camisole over my head. He pushed me gently on the bed and removed his jeans. He unzipped mine and pulled them down my legs. *Was this really happening to me?*

He climbed on top of me, looked into my eyes, and began kissing me, at first soft and sweet. Then his mouth covered mine, with deep, passionate kisses. It was like eating your favorite flavor ice cream cone, lick by lick. I snuggled my head into his neck and took in his strong scent. He looked down at me, closed his eyes, and began kissing me again. He was artful in his lovemaking. The motion of his body was like a fine-tuned instrument. I rolled on top of him, my rose-gold heart hanging in front of that amazing face. I could feel every part of my body responding to his touch. He was forceful and intense yet so loving. He was demanding yet gentle. He knew exactly what he wanted and how to get it. He also knew how to pleasure a woman. He was more than willing to please. So was I.

I awoke close to four in the morning. I slept like a baby. Ethan was sitting on the couch in his jeans, no shirt. He had a drink in his hand. I wrapped the sheet around my naked body and walked to the couch and sat beside him. I ran my hand along the scar on his side.

"This must have been terrible for you."

He moved my hand away. "It was, but not as bad as the men who were killed. It was a car bomb on the side of the road. No one saw it coming. We lost four men. I was one of the so-called lucky ones."

I was very surprised he started to share this information with me.

"It took a long time for my body to heal. The mind never forgets. I knew the risks I would be taking when I joined." He went on, "That was one of the reasons I never had a serious relationship with a woman. I wouldn't want to marry and leave a wife or girlfriend behind, especially with my baby."

I could see now why he didn't care if I was married or not. He had no intention of a relationship. He just needed to be with someone for a night. He needed to hold someone for a while. It made me feel so sorry for him. He was such a beautiful man, so lost and alone. I wanted to be with him for now. I wanted to comfort him, make love to him. To make him feel someone cared. I knew I only had a couple of hours left before I would leave him, and that would be that. I should go home where I belong. I hoped that this one crazy night would now relieve my fantasy and let me get him out of my mind. I had no intentions of having an affair. I had my Jake. We spoke a while longer when I told him it was time for me to go home. I went in the bathroom, took a quick shower, and dressed. He offered me a cup of coffee, but I declined. I took my cell from my purse and arranged for a cab. I asked him for the address of the building, since I hadn't noticed it when we arrived the night before. I gave it to the dispatcher on the phone.

It felt so strange to leave him, but I knew I had to go. Jake would be waiting for me at home. As I approached the door, he called, "Elizabeth, can I see you again?" I turned, surprised.

"Ethan, tonight was beautiful, amazing actually, but you know I'm married. I can't let this happen again."

He called to me again, "Elizabeth, please, this is the most I felt like a whole man in a long time. It's taken me a while to be with a woman again, and you are just so, I don't know, well you're just you, easy to be with. You make me feel comfortable, please, Liz. I know you're married. No strings, I promise." He called me Liz.

My eyes started to fill. I wrote my cell number on the Macy's receipt that was still in my bag from this afternoon, the one for the Chanel lipstick, handed it to him, and walked out the door. I got into the cab and started to cry. I gave the driver my address and prayed that I could forgive myself and not break down into tears of guilt when I got home and faced Jake.

Jake was still in bed asleep. I quietly opened the door to the bedroom and checked on him. He was curled up on his side of the bed, my side obviously neat. I went to the kitchen and made a pot of coffee. I sat at the island and waited for Jake to wake up. He came into the kitchen a while later stretching.

"I thought I smelled fresh coffee. Hi, Kid. How's your dad?"

All I could say was "Fine."

"Emma, it's supposed to be a beautiful weekend. I thought we might take a drive to the house in the Hamptons. I could use some quiet time. We could relax and have a nice dinner. What do you say?" He poured a cup of coffee and gave me a kiss on the cheek.

Oh god, not this weekend. Not after last night.

"Jake, I'm feeling a little under the weather this morning. Can we please do it another time?"

He gave me a little bump with his hip. "Come on, Kid. The ride and fresh air will do you some good."

What could I say to him? I felt so guilty I wanted to vomit. Saying no to Jake would only make me feel worse. I agreed to go.

My mind rushed back to the time when we bought the house. It was shortly after I had my last miscarriage. Jake felt the house would give me something to focus on, painting, redecorating, and buying new furniture. He said that I needed a change of scenery. I needed something to distract me. I was so depressed. He was the doctor. He was right. It did help me feel better. It would never cure the ache in my heart, nothing ever could, but I did love this house. It wasn't a huge mansion, like some homes you see in the Hamptons. It was more of a country cottage with a beautiful wraparound porch and swing. It had a large bay window in the living room overlooking the beach and the road that led to the house. A lovely country kitchen let the morning sunshine in. It had three bedrooms upstairs. The master bedroom, which I had done in a shabby chic French décor. The second bedroom, Jake used as an office. The third one was a little smaller. We used that one for storage. One day, it might have been a nursery, but that wasn't going to happen. I could barely bring myself to open the door to that room.

Jake and I left about 10:00 a.m. I put my head back on the leather headrest and tried to fall asleep, but my mind kept drifting to the night before. How would I feel right now if Ethan was driving this car? What if I was going away to spend the weekend with him? We could make love all weekend, walk on the beach, and sit on the front porch swing and watch the sunset.

Stop it, Emma. Stop it right now.

Jake turned his head and smiled at me. "I love you, Kid."

I smiled back at him and rubbed his arm. How can I love one man with all my heart and yet be so obsessed with another? I enjoyed making love to Jake. It was romantic and affectionate, and it always gave me pleasure. Yet Ethan showed me another side. It was wildly intense; it wasn't lovemaking, it was pure sex. It, too, gave me great pleasure. I looked out the window of the car, not knowing how to feel. I put my head back and drifted off to sleep.

Jake and I had many happy years at this cottage. During the summer, many of the library programs would be closed because of the number of children who would go off to summer camps. So I had plenty of time off. Jake would clear his calendar for a few weeks, and we would take a relaxing vacation. We would invite friends on weekends and stay up to all hours of the night, talking and playing games. It was fun. My dad would enjoy coming up on occasion and tinker around the house doing odd jobs. He sort of made it his little weekend hobby. The best times, though, were when Jake and I were alone. We had quiet dinners on the back deck, followed by walks on the beach. It took me a while to get used to the idea that I was not trying to get pregnant every time we made love. It made me feel a little empty inside, but Jake comforted me by saying we should just relax and enjoy each other. He would assure me that I was all he needed and wanted. Being in such a beautiful, peaceful environment and Jake's patience and understanding helped tremendously, that first summer, in our little cottage.

Now I'm thinking what it would be like to spend time in our peaceful sanctuary with Ethan.

It was just a fantasy I kept telling myself.

That night, Jake and I went to our favorite seafood restaurant nearby and had a delicious lobster dinner. He told me about some of his patient's cases and the horrific stories they had told him, but again, he was very careful not to divulge names. *They were similar to what Ethan had told me. I listened and thought to myself, was that what Ethan had gone through? Did he need a psychiatrist? Was it possible he was one of Jake's troubled patients? In the middle of dinner, my cell went off.*

Chapter 7

At first, I didn't answer it. I told Jake it was Dad. I would call him back later. We were in the middle of dinner, and I didn't want to interrupt our conversation. In truth, I didn't recognize the number. On the way back to the cottage, the cell went off again. Jake told me to answer the call, that it might be something important, I hesitated, but I did as he suggested and answered. I recognized Ethan's voice and had to pretend it was someone else.

"Hello, Dad, everything okay?"

"Dad? I take it you can't talk right now."

"That's right, I was in the middle of dinner. I'm sorry, Dad. I forgot to call when I got home this morning. We decided to take a ride to the cottage in Southampton. It was a last-minute thing," I said *we*, being so careful not to use Jake's name. I didn't want him to know my husband's name or anything else about him for that matter.

"I didn't mean to worry you. I'm a married woman you know, Dad." I emphasized "married" into the phone.

"Did you say cottage in Southampton?" Ethan's voice was inquisitive.

"We are on our way home to go to bed." *Point made.* "I'll talk to you during the week. Love you, Bye, Dad".

"Love me, do you?" Ethan's voice was playful. I hung up.

Oh god, I shouldn't have said that. Would Ethan think I meant that for him? I had to make it sound as if I was talking my father.

I told Jake that he was concerned when I didn't answer the first time, so he called back. Jake shook his head and laughed. "Emma, you just left him this morning. He has to calm down. He'll give himself a heart attack."

"I know, but he is still such a worrier. I told him I would call when I got home and then you mentioned coming out here, I totally forgot. Of course, when he didn't hear from me by tonight, he started to panic, you know how he is."

We pulled into the driveway, and I was glad to be out of the car. I didn't want to talk about my father anymore, knowing full well it wasn't really him on the phone. I felt so deceitful. I shut my cell and put it in my handbag. Hearing Ethan's voice excited yet unnerved me. I sat on the porch swing and told Jake I needed to get some fresh air. There was a cool breeze blowing off the water, and it felt so good against my skin. I closed my eyes and rocked back and forth.

"Don't be too long, Kid. I'm going up."

I sat there and stared at the waves rolling in on the shore. That's how my mind felt, like the waves beating against the rocks. *I made a mistake. I won't make it again. I can't.*

I climbed the stairs and walked into the bedroom. Jake was already in bed, naked. I couldn't say no. Not here, not now. This was our sanctuary. I got undressed and slid into bed next to him. He turned to face me.

"I love being here with you, Emma. These are the best days of my life. I love you."

"I love you too, Jake." *I did. I really did.*

He rolled on top and me and slid one hand under my waist. His other hand reached for mine and held it tightly. He kissed me slowly, his mouth covering mine, and started to thrust. I gasped in discomfort. He took my gasp as a sign of pleasure, and it excited him even more. He couldn't have been more wrong. My eyes filled with tears, partially from the discomfort in my body from the night before with Ethan, and the guilty ache in my heart for betraying Jake. I didn't realize how forceful Ethan had been; it was as if he was fighting his own internal demons and expressing it through his body. It wasn't until Jake and I started to make love that I realized how forceful Ethan had been, causing my discomfort. I closed my eyes and held on to Jake, letting him make love to his wife. I owed him that much. When Jake fell asleep, I went into the bathroom and ran a warm bath. I sat in the tub for a while to soothe my body.

Sunday was a quiet day. We had coffee and bagels for breakfast; we sat and watched some of the Sunday morning news shows. Jake decided to take a walk on the beach. I threw on a pair of sweats, went in Jake's office, and found a book on post-traumatic stress disorder. I was curious as to whether physical aggression, in any form, was part of what Ethan was being treated for. I sat on the porch swing and started to read.

I looked in the glossary under PTSD. It read: a disorder that occurs following an extreme traumatic stress in which a person shows symptoms of reexperiencing an event, avoiding reminders of the trauma, and of persistent symptoms of increased arousal. Could it be that when Ethan had sex, he was fighting his inner demons and the enemy all over again? It didn't seem that way to me. He just seemed very intense and passionate. He needed some compassion; he needed to be loved so he could put the misery in his life behind him. He felt the need to hold onto someone, even if it was for only an hour or a day. I didn't know if I should call him back. How could that possibly help?

He was so beautiful and yet so emotionally damaged.

Jake and I drove home and hit hours of traffic. I sat in the car thinking about what I should do or should not do. I was totally confused. When I got home, I turned my phone back on and found my decision had been made for me. There was one message from my father, just checking in. There were three messages from Ethan to please give him a call back when I got home. I decided to call Ethan, but that would have to wait till the morning. I was exhausted, confused, and I really didn't know what to say to him. *"Oh, Ethan, I'm married, I love my husband. I can't do this to him." Or "I think you're really hot and we had amazing sex, we should definitely do it again sometime." But then again, maybe not.*

I took a quick shower and climbed into bed. I was dreading the morning. Jake watched the eleven evening news, and I was sound asleep by the time he came to bed. In the morning, Jake was already having coffee when I walked into the kitchen. He was leaving for the office in a few minutes. He had an early day.

"Thanks again for a great weekend, Kid." He gave me a quick kiss and headed for the door.

"Have a good day, Jake, love you."

I hope he has a better day than the one I was about to have. I'll wait a little while and make my phone call.

It was about noon when I got the courage to check my phone for Ethan's phone number. I tapped the number with my finger and prayed it would go straight to voicemail. At least I can say I returned the call and not actually have to speak to him. I still didn't know what to say. The cell rang.

"Ethan."

My god he answered.

"Hi, it's Elizabeth. I'm returning your calls." That was fairly easy.

"How was your weekend at the, what did you call it, the cottage?" His voice was cold.

"Do I sense sarcasm, Ethan? It was very enjoyable, actually. Thank you."

I was annoyed at the tone in his voice. He didn't really know me. How dare he take that attitude?

"I'm sorry, Elizabeth, I just wanted to see you."

"Ethan, really, you know I'm a happily married woman. What happened between us should not have happened at all, it's that simple."

"Happily, did you say happily married? That's funny because a happily married woman wouldn't have left the bar with me and gone to my place knowing what was about to happen. For that matter, you wouldn't have called me back." He went on, "As a matter of fact, why did you call, Elizabeth? I'll tell you why. You called me back because you know you want to see me again. You want to be with me. You enjoyed every minute of it. Admit it. We were great together. You know it, and I know it."

But I was happily married. It was just a moment of letting a fantasy take over.

I hung up. I shouldn't have called back. I shouldn't have given him the satisfaction. The truth was he was right I did want to see him. I wanted to see him so badly it hurt. My cell rang again. It was him. I didn't answer. It rang again. I hesitated, but this time, I did pick up, "Yes, Ethan." My voice was barely a whisper.

"Meet me tomorrow, Liz, please."

I didn't answer for a moment. I didn't know how to respond to him, but I knew I needed to put an end to this.

"Fine, we need to have a serious talk, Ethan."

"I'll be at the promenade in Brooklyn Heights at 11:00 a.m."

I thought it best to get out of the city and to meet someplace where things couldn't get too involved. I said goodbye, turned off my phone, and put it in my handbag.

Will I show up tomorrow? Hell if I know.

I did decide to go to Brooklyn Heights after all; why, I wasn't sure. I should leave well enough alone. Just call Ethan and say have a nice day, have a nice life. But I just couldn't. I stopped at Starbucks on my way to the R train and ordered a Grande red eye chai tea. I was going to take my car, but the parking in the Heights was such a nuisance. I figured the train would be a lot easier and faster, no traffic. I got off the train around ten forty-five at the corner of Montague and Court Streets and walked down to the promenade. I looked around but didn't see Ethan. Maybe, he chose not to come. I'll wait a little while. If he's not here within the hour, I'll just leave. I walked along the promenade and sat on a bench.

The New York skyline in lower Manhattan looked so majestic. No hint of the tragedy that took place on 9/11. I was only twenty-two on that infamous day when the towers fell, but I remembered it like it was yesterday. When I met Jake a year later and we discussed the events of that day, he told me about the number of patients he had seen who suffered from the tragedy. People who lost someone and families who never knew what exactly had happened to their loved ones. No remains to bury for closure, no place to go and mourn. Not until that beautiful memorial, at the Freedom Tower, was built. Now people from all over can come and visit and pay their respects.

I looked at my watch; it was eleven fifteen. I was deep in thought and hadn't realized the time was passing. I looked around for Ethan; he was nowhere in sight. I stood up and started to walk back to the train. I was a little relieved and a little disappointed that he never showed up. I went down the subway steps and waited on the platform for the R train going toward Manhattan. The train pulled in the station. I sat down and looked out the window. The R train coming in from Manhattan was leaving the station just as I sat, and there on the opposite platform was Ethan heading up the stairs to the street. He was coming to meet me after all. My heart started to race. He really did have an effect on me. In my excitement, I started tapping on the window, knowing full well he couldn't possibly hear me with the roar of the moving train. I sat back stunned as the train pulled out of the station.

I said I would give it an hour, why did I leave after fifteen minutes? Maybe fate was trying to tell me something; I didn't really know. Should I get off at the next station and go back? Should I call and tell him I was there or just let him wonder?

Chapter 8

I stopped at the library on my way home from the promenade to see when my next scheduled date was due. I wasn't due back in until Wednesday afternoon at two. So that gave me a whole free day on Tuesday. I spoke to Jake at the office and asked him what time he would be home and what he would like to do for dinner. He said he should be home about six, and we can decide on dinner when he got in.

That was perfectly fine with me. I certainly did not feel like cooking. I didn't even want to cut up veggies for a salad. I was still a little shaken about seeing Ethan in the subway. I'm sure that he was on his way to meet me, if only I would have waited a little longer. I sat on the couch with a glass of white wine and turned on the TV. I just flipped channels, but nothing caught my attention. I turned it off. I was staring out the window, not really looking at anything in particular, when my cell went off. I looked at the number. It was Ethan.

"Hello, Liz, it's Ethan." His voice sounded jaded. I'm glad he called and didn't text. I like to hear a person's voice when they call; I always did. I want to hear the tone of their voices so I know what type of conversation we were about to have. In this case, I could tell he was not happy with how today's events had gone.

"Hi, Ethan."

I thought about how I felt when I saw him standing on the platform. *Those sad blue eyes that said so much and yet said nothing.* The scar running down his body, which made me think of the kind of hell he must have endured on his tours overseas. The damage he suffered mentally. I felt a pang of sympathy for him. I was just about to tell him I was sorry I had just missed him in the subway, and that I had seen him on the station platform when he started talking.

"Sorry I couldn't make it today, Liz, something else came up. Maybe we can get together another time or not."

Oh, so he wanted to play that game, did he. He thought I stood him up, so he was deliberately being indifferent. Well, two can play at that game. I really didn't want to do this, but I felt as if I was being put on the defensive. He obviously didn't take rejection or being stood up very well.

"Well, to be perfectly honest, Ethan, I wasn't too sure it was such a good idea for me to come either. Sorry."

There was a dead silence on the other end. I didn't know what else to say. I should have just said, "Stop it, Ethan, I saw you on the subway platform as I was leaving on the train going back to the city. We just missed each other. That's all." But I didn't. I just couldn't say it. Let him think that I didn't show up. He wanted me to think he rejected me, fine. I'll play along with his game as childish as it may be.

"Okay, well then, bye, Ethan." I listened for a moment.

"Take care, Liz." The phone went dead.

I had a late dinner with Jake; we sent for Chinese. Jake stayed up and watched the evening news. I told him I had an awful headache and went to bed. I couldn't sleep all night, tossing and turning. I kept seeing Ethan standing on the platform. He was coming to meet me, and I went there as well. We did want to see each other. Why play such a childish game? I knew what I needed to do tomorrow. I just couldn't leave things this way.

In retrospect, I most certainly should have.

Wednesday morning was rainy and dreary. The sky was gray. I looked at all the little people on the streets below rushing to work, their umbrellas perched over their heads. I was glad I didn't have to be at the library until two. Hopefully, it would clear up by then. I turned on the early morning news to check the weather. Rain, rain, and more rain all day. I thought of Ethan sitting in his neat little studio apartment watching the rain.

How nice it would be to spend a rainy day like this in bed with him. Just lying there with no place to go and nothing to do except be with each other.

I wanted to call him and say that I'll be there in five minutes, be ready, but I had the library at two, and in all honesty, I didn't know how he would react to me going to his apartment after our not-so-pleasant conversation. I'll wait a day or two and give him a call back. Hopefully, his attitude would have changed by then, and we could have a civil conversation. Just then, my phone rang, and I jumped.

"Hello?" I didn't even look at the number to see who it was; I was so startled.

"Come over now. I need to see you." It was Ethan's voice.

I rested the phone against my chest and took a deep breath. "What's your address again, Ethan? I'll be there in an hour or so."

I hung up and ran into the bathroom. I took a quick shower, blew my hair, and put on jeans and a cami. I didn't expect to be wearing them very long. I rode the elevator down to the garage level in the building and got in my car. Today was not a day to walk to the train, even with an umbrella. I got in my BMW and headed downtown. Traffic was crazy this time of day, rush hour was crazy. This only made me more anxious. It took me almost forty-five minutes to get to his building, and finding a parking spot was no easy task either.

By the time I walked the three blocks from my car to his building, I was soaked. I ran up the small stoop and rang the bell. He didn't even ask who was at the door; he just buzzed me in. I opened the door; the little black-and-white tile floor looking so familiar. The smell of fresh paint had faded. The second door buzzed, and I ran up to the second floor and knocked on his door. Ethan let me in. *Oh my god.* He had just stepped out of the shower. Towel wrapped around his hips. His body gleaming with small beads of water and his wet hair pushed back with his fingers. The fresh scent of his body wash was intoxicating. Any woman would be envious of me standing here, looking at this amazing man. He started walking toward me.

"You're all wet," he whispered.

Believe me, you have no idea. When he was a breath's distance away from me, the towel fell. He was most definitely happy to see me. He made me feel like I was spinning out of control. Being with him was like being in another realm. Each moment was more exciting than the last. And so my body's feelings overshadowed what I knew was right in my heart. I was supposed to tell him goodbye.

I didn't want to leave, but I had to be at the library by two. I had no choice. I would love to just stay in bed, next to him, all day. I looked at that sleeping face and gave him a little kiss on his ear. I started to get up when he stirred.

"Do you have to leave already? You know, three is my lucky number." He smiled and pulled me back into the bed.

"Oh really, three? And as much as I would love to stay, I really do have to go."

He let go of my arm and said nothing. It was very obvious he didn't want to be alone. Could it be part of his PTSD? Not liking the feeling of being left alone. I went into the bathroom and took a quick shower. My clothes were almost dry. Ethan had put them over the chair by the kitchen table after he removed them. It didn't matter if my hair was still a little damp when I got to the library; after all, I had just come in out of the rain.

"When can I see you again, Liz?"

"Maybe Friday night. My husband sometimes works late on Fridays."

But, honestly, I wasn't even sure if I would be available to do that. I had no idea what Jake might have planned for us on Friday. I was still careful not to use Jake's name or his profession.

"I can't on Friday night, Liz, I have an appointment. I hate this not being able to see you." He got out of bed and put on his jeans. He walked to the kitchen and poured himself a drink. I thought of Dean's drinking habits, and I hoped Ethan wasn't going down that same path.

"Saturday then. I promise Saturday, I'll call you on Friday and give you a definite time. I promise, Ethan." I walked out the door feeling like I had just left an abandoned baby on church steps.

I got to the library just about two. I shook out my umbrella and headed to the children's section. Not too many children were at the library today. Some children were still on vacation or at camp. I'm sure a number of parents decided to stay in with this terrible weather. There were the Murphy twins—two adorable, blue-eyed little boys, about age four—Michael and Max sitting on the floor waiting. Their mother, Courtney, an attractive blond, was on a chair nearby.

She was always a pleasure to talk to, and the boys were very well-behaved. Lily and Molly were waiting with their mom, Sara, as well. Lily was almost five and Molly three. Sara had a little bump below her belly button.

Could she be pregnant again or just gaining a few pounds? I really couldn't tell, and I wasn't about to ask. That was the kids for today. That should make the day go a whole lot easier on me.

I took out a science book about how rain forms for their age level, and started to read. As usual, they had a million questions. How do clouds stay in the sky? Why is rain wet? Why do puddles dry when the sun comes out? Today was the perfect day for a lesson on how rain was formed, and I answered their little questions as best as I could. When we were done reading, I took out some craft paper and helped them make colorful paper umbrellas, which, I'm positive, will never make it to their homes in one piece. They always like to empty out a bottle of glue on their project, but nothing ever stays together. As we finished our colorful umbrellas, little Lily came up to me and pulled on my arm.

"Yes, Lily, how can I help you, sweetheart?" I asked.

"Ms. Emma," she said in her sweet little voice, "where is your pretty heart necklace? You know, the one you always wear around your neck? You wear it every day. Why don't you have it on today? I just love it." She smiled.

I put my hand to my neck and felt nothing. I thought I would faint. It must have come undone when Ethan pulled my shirt over my head. Maybe, the clasp caught on the shirt. It has to be at his apartment. That was the only place it could be. I knew I put it on when I was getting dressed this morning.

I excused myself and ran into the bathroom. I called Ethan and prayed that he would answer. *Please, pick up, Ethan, please.*

"Liz, what's up?" His voice sounded confused. I had just left him a couple of hours ago.

"Ethan, can you please check your apartment for my rose-gold heart? One of the children noticed I wasn't wearing it. I didn't even realize it was gone. Your apartment can be the only place I left it. When you took off my shirt, it must have come undone. Please, check, Ethan, it's very important. I feel sick. I'll die if I lose it."

"Calm down, Liz, give me a few minutes. I'll call you back." He hung up.

I waited and prayed in what felt like an eternity. My phone rang.

"The necklace is here. It was under the kitchen chair where I put your clothes to dry. I'll give it to you on Saturday. I'll put it on my nightstand. Calm down, Liz, it's fine."

"Oh, thank God. Thank you, Ethan. I'll see you Saturday." I took a deep breath and began to relax.

Ethan almost sounded a little jealous that I was so upset over missing the heart that my husband had given me. Oh my god, Jake. Jake will notice I'm not wearing it. What do I tell Jake? I'll say that the clasp felt loose and I took it to the jeweler to have it repaired. They told me to come back on Saturday, that it would be finished. Another lie. This will give me the perfect excuse to go out and go to Ethan's, pick up the necklace, and spend the afternoon.

That evening, I made a nice dinner for Jake. It's funny what guilt will make you do. A roast, with all the trimmings, was cooking in the oven. It actually came pretty good. I surprised myself. I had wine, candles, and some romantic music playing in the background.

My dad and I always liked Frank Sinatra and Dean Martin. I still enjoyed listening to them. Jake came home around seven.

"Something smells really good, Kid. Okay, let's hear it, how much did you spend today?" He laughed.

"Nothing honestly, and you know you wouldn't be angry even if I did. I just felt like doing something nice for my hardworking, brilliant husband."

I asked him how his day went, and he gave me hints of this and that, but nothing really he could talk about. These were the hazards of his profession. He did mention, however, one captain who had been having a particularly rough time opening up to him. He lost a number of men under his command and was seriously injured himself. He was quite concerned about him. Then he noticed, looking at my neck.

"Emma, where's your heart?"

I explained that when I was getting dressed, *or undressed as the case may be,* the clasp felt loose, and I brought it to the jewelers to have it fixed. It will be ready on Saturday, around one. He seemed to accept this explanation just fine. Why wouldn't he? He had no reason to doubt me. He had no reason not to trust me, which made it all the more upsetting to me. He trusted me implicitly. We began to eat dinner and have a nice, relaxing evening, sipping our wine and listening to the music I had put in the CD player. *I did love this man.*

He stood up from the dinner table, put out his hand, and asked, "Shall we dance, Kid?"

Dean Martin was signing in the background, "Everybody Loves Somebody, Sometime." It was one of my all-time favorites. My mom and I would clean our house on a Saturday morning and dance to these songs. I loved those times. My friends would be listening to crazy rock bands, and I would be listening to my dad's albums on his stereo in the living room. My mother especially loved Dean's olive oil voice, as the Italians would call it. She would always say that he made her swoon. I reached for Jake's outstretched hand.

"Why, Doctor, I would love to." I put down my wine and stood up. I wrapped my arms around his neck and squeezed tight as if I never wanted to let go.

I rested my head on his shoulder and snuggled into his neck. I could feel my eyes begin to tear.

Is it possible for one woman to love one man so deeply, with her whole heart and soul, and yet be so physically attracted to another? Does the body have so much more power over the heart and mind? I wish I had the answer. I wish I could understand.

There was only one conclusion I could think of. I'll pick up my heart on Saturday afternoon, wish Ethan well, and get on with my life. I'll hope, beyond hope, that Jake never finds out how foolish I have been. I have a good life with Jake; I am not going to destroy it.

Chapter 9

Friday morning, before Jake left for work, he asked me if I would like to meet him after his last appointment of the day. Maybe, we could have a bite to eat and take a drive to the Hamptons. He wanted to get away for the weekend. He needed the rest; he had a very long week. I said absolutely, I would love to. I would pack a small bag for us and pick him up at his office. I told him to call me an hour before he was expected to be finished with his last patient. This would give me time to get to the office. All plans were set in motion until I remembered my heart.

"Oh Jake, I can't. I have to pick up my heart tomorrow at the jewelers." I told Ethan I would be there. "I'm so sorry."

I could tell Jake was disappointed. "Emma, really, can't that wait a few days? It's not going to disappear. You can get the heart on Monday or Tuesday."

Of course, Jake was right, but what do I tell Ethan?

I did want to tell Ethan goodbye and move on. If I don't show up tomorrow, I know he'll call. What a mess I created for myself. How do I know Ethan won't do something with the heart, like dump it in the nearest trash can? I see how he reacts when he thinks he's being rejected. I have to figure something out.

"You're right, Jake, I'll get it Tuesday. Call me later and tell me what time to pick you up."

"Thanks, Emma, I really need the break. See you later, Kid." He left for the office.

Emma, think. How are you going to get yourself out of this situation? Call Ethan, go to his apartment, and pick up the heart now. I'll explain to him that I just can't risk my marriage for an afternoon of sex. Any woman would be lucky to have him in her life. I'll hold my ground even if he persists. I'll just leave. I'll tell Jake the jewelers called to tell me the heart was ready today. I'll resume my life. Get back to normal.

I called Ethan and got no answer. I'll try again later. I went in the bedroom closet and pulled out my overnight bag. I'll pack a few things for me and Jake. We have plenty of things we'll need at the cottage. Maybe, I'll call Cathy, our housekeeper out there, and ask her just to freshen up the house a little. I tried Ethan again and again, there was no answer. What's up? I started to get concerned. I called Cathy and asked her if she was available to do a light cleaning this afternoon.

"No problem, Mrs. Farrell, have a safe trip out."

"Great, thanks, Cathy, you're the best. Bye."

Again, I tried Ethan. Again, there was no answer.

At eleven, Jake called. "Hi, Jake, I was just getting our bag ready. What time do you want to leave tonight?"

I was praying he would say late so I would have time to get Ethan's before we left and pick up my heart.

"I'm sorry, Emma, I can't go."

I was totally surprised. "You can't go? Why not, what's wrong? Jake, are you all right?"

"I'm fine. I just received a phone call from the veteran's hospital. One of my patients, the captain I told you about, was brought in to the emergency room. The doctor found my business card in his wallet, along with his military ID card. No other contacts were found in the wallet, except for a crumbled-up Macy's receipt with a faded phone number on the back, which couldn't be read. It was obviously a woman's receipt. It was for a lipstick. His phone might have had other important numbers, but wasn't on him when the ambulance brought him in. It must have fallen out of his pocket or hand when he tried to help the girl. He could have been calling 911. The doctor told me, apparently, last night, he was leaving a bistro not far from my office when he saw a young girl being harassed by two men. Being who he is, the quintessential marine, he tried to help her.

"The two men attacked him. They hit him on the side of the head with a pistol. He fell and hit the back of his head on the curb. He's in pretty bad condition. The girl was beaten around the face. Her clothes were torn, and she had bruises on her arms and breasts. If he hadn't intervened, she might have been raped or even killed. Patrons in the bistro heard screams and came out. They saw the altercation and called the police. They explained what had happened. The two men ran away. She was brought to NYU and is expected to be okay, but she's badly shaken up. The captain's unconscious. That's all I know right now. Doctors are doing tests. I want to go to the hospital and see what's going on. I have a responsibility to him. I told you, he never really opened up to me, so I don't know much about his family life. I don't even know if there is anyone we should contact. I only know what he told me about the military. I'm sure they must have records for his next of kin and family members. I'll look into it."

"Jake, can I meet you at the hospital? I don't want you to go alone," I insisted. I was starting to get this overwhelming feeling that something wasn't right. Could the patient in the ER be Ethan? So many things made it seem that way: he was a marine under Jake's care, the Macy's receipt in his wallet, I hadn't been able to get in touch with Ethan all day. Helping a young woman being attacked seemed like something Ethan would do. The bistro was near Jake's office. What are the odds? Jake was talking in the background."

"No, Emma, I'm already on my way. I'll call you in a little while and let you know what time I'll be home. Sorry about the weekend, Kid."

I was barely listening to him. "No problem, see you later. Jake, wait, what's the marine's name? Can you at least tell me that?" I asked, not knowing why I had this overwhelming feeling of dread.

"Ethan, Capt. Ethan Miller." He hung up.

Chapter 10

I dropped the phone. My body began to shake all over.

I'm being punished for having an affair. And Ethan is being punished for sleeping with a married woman.

I tried to walk into the bathroom, swaying back and forth. My head was spinning and I thought I would hit the floor. I knelt over the toilet and began vomiting. I tried to lean against the bathroom wall but slid down. *Ethan, why did this have to happen to Ethan?*

I sat there for what felt like an eternity, waiting for Jake to call me back and tell me what was happening at the hospital. I couldn't take it anymore. I stood up, went to the sink, and washed my face. *I'm going to the hospital and see him. I want to be there. What if he dies? Oh god, he can't die. There will be no family there for him.* I went back to the toilet and threw up again.

I'll just tell Jake that I wanted to come for support. What can he do once I'm there? Throw me out?

I grabbed my bag, took the elevator down to the street, went outside, and hailed a cab. The whole time I was in the cab, I was praying for God to help Ethan. *He's been through so much already. You have to help him.* My head was spinning, a million thoughts going through my mind.

Why was he at the bistro in the middle of the night? He has to be all right. Please, let him be all right.

I asked the cab driver to drop me off by the emergency room. I walked through the glass doors. It felt like I was walking in slow motion, one heavy step after another. I couldn't breathe.

Come on, Emma, you can do this.

I was so terrified of what I would hear. I felt like I was living in a nightmare. *But I'm not going to wake up from this one. How do I get my heart from Ethan's apartment? What do I tell Jake?* My mind was racing in a million directions. I walked over to the nurse's station. My face must have had anxiety written all over it because she asked, "Are you all right, miss?"

I half smiled. "I'm here to inquire about a friend. He was brought in during the night. Ethan Miller." My voice was barely a whisper.

"I'm sorry, I can't give out any information unless it's family."

I stared at her with complete fear on my face. "Please," I whispered.

She looked at me, knowing he had to be more than a friend. She could see the distraught look on my face. She looked on her computer. She spoke in a soft voice, "I can tell by the way you look you're very upset. All I can say is that he's in ICU on the tenth floor."

I walked around to the main lobby and stepped on the elevator. My mind flashed back to the day I bumped into Ethan getting off the elevator. I hadn't known his name then. No one else was in the elevator, so it went straight to the tenth floor. Thank God. The doors opened. A sign on the wall in front of me read ICU, with an arrow pointing to the right. I started walking that way when I saw Jake talking to the doctor. His back was to me, but then the doctor looked up and asked if I needed assistance. Jake turned around and was surprised to see me. He seemed so frustrated.

"Emma, what are you doing here? Doctor, this is my wife, Emma. I thought you were going to wait at home. I told you I would call when I had some information. You shouldn't upset yourself with this."

I was annoyed at Jake's attitude. I knew that he was very upset, but that was no reason for him to act like such a shit. That totally wasn't his personality, especially when it came to me.

"I just wanted to be here for you and see how your patient was doing, or maybe you wanted to get something to eat when you were done here. That's all, really."

Jake seemed to change his tone a little. Perhaps he is just worried about Ethan, too. "He's still unconscious. The doctors did a brain scan. He has a concussion, but he doesn't have any serious brain trauma. They're still waiting for him to regain consciousness." Jake started to walk me back to the elevator. Ironically, this whole mess began with a bump in an elevator. "Go home, Emma, please. I'll be there in a little while. I just want to stay a little longer to see if he regains consciousness. There isn't anything you can do here, and I'm really not in the mood for anything to eat. Thanks anyway."

I got in the elevator, and the doors closed. *So I am getting thrown out after all. I guess I won't see Ethan today. But you can be sure I'll be back tomorrow, with or without Jake.*

I calmed down considerably when I got home, now that I knew there were no serious injuries to Ethan's head. I poured myself a glass of wine and threw myself on the bed. I started coming to my senses. What if he woke up and recognized me, especially with Jake standing in the room? *How would I explain that?* I would have told the truth. I bumped into him in the lobby of Jake's building, and he might have remembered me. No need for further explanation.

I still needed to figure out how I can get my heart from his apartment. Maybe, there's a superintendent that could let me in. I could tell him I needed to pick up some things for Ethan, who is in the hospital. I put my head back on the pillow and fell asleep. I was emotionally exhausted. Jake came in around nine. The sound of the bedroom door opening woke me. At first, I was going to pretend I was still sleeping, but I had to know.

I rolled over and asked, "How is he?"

"He's still unconscious but stable. Go back to sleep, Kid. We'll talk in the morning."

I rolled over and closed my eyes.

I woke up early on Saturday. Jake was still sleeping. I decided to go to Ethan's apartment building and see if there was a superintendent available that would let me in. I didn't bother to wake Jake. I just left. I was still surprised at his attitude regarding my appearance at the hospital yesterday. Maybe, if it was someone else, I wouldn't have been as worried as I was, but this was Ethan. Obviously, Jake didn't know why I was so concerned. I got that, and I understood why Jake was so stressed. He couldn't help Dean and now Ethan was in the hospital. But Ethan didn't drive himself off a road while drunk; he was trying to help some poor girl who was being attacked. It was not the same situation at all, surely Jake must understand that. But he felt responsible for Ethan the way he did for Dean.

I hailed a cab and went to Ethan's building. I rang the first-floor bell. No one answered. It was only eight fifteen in the morning on Saturday. These people weren't going to be happy with me, that's for damn sure. I didn't care; I rang the bell again. A young woman's voice came over the intercom.

"Yes, can I help you? You do know it's Saturday morning, and it's not even 9:00 a.m. Some of us work all week."

"Yes, I do, and I am sorry. My name is Liz. I'm a friend of Ethan on the second floor. He's in the hospital. He was pretty badly injured last night. He was trying to help a young woman who was being attacked by two men." I knew I was giving too much information, but I was trying to plead on her sympathy. It worked too.

The door opened, and she stepped out pulling on a robe. She was a pretty little blond. "Oh, I'm so sorry to hear that. He's such a nice guy. Hot too. How can I help?"

"Well, I was wondering if there was a superintendent for the building who can let me in his apartment. I'd like to get some things Ethan might need at the hospital. You know, a comb, razor, toothbrush, basic things."

She shook her head. "I'm sorry, there is no super on the premises. The owner of the building lives in Westchester. He sends maintenance people once a month or when someone needs repair work done. That's basically it. I'm really sorry. I wish I could be of more help. Please tell Ethan Suzanne on the first floor hopes he's feeling better real soon. I'd love to make him a nice home-cooked meal." She winked.

I started down the stoop. My gold heart was still sitting on his nightstand. I turned and called back to Suzanne. She stopped at her door. *I prayed she had an understanding heart.* "If I give you my phone number, can you call me and let me know if maintenance workers or the landlord come by the building? Maybe they'll let me in the apartment."

She thought for a minute then looked at me and smiled. "This isn't about toiletries, is it? You can get them in any drugstore. You left something important behind. There's something you need to get, something that will be missed. I get it. Sure, give me your number."

I wrote my number on a small piece of paper and handed it to her. "Thank you. You don't know how much this means to me."

She took the paper. "I'll do my best."

What if the super hears about Ethan, goes into the apartment to make sure everything is in order, and finds my heart? He might hand it over to the police because Ethan was assaulted. They might question who it could belong to and who might have left the heart behind. With my initials in the heart and my husband his doctor, it wouldn't take a genius long to figure it out. If they showed it to Jake, he would know it was mine immediately. I'm really being punished for my sins, I knew it.

I grabbed another cab and went over to the VA hospital. This time, I took the elevator right up to the tenth floor and walked casually to the nurses' station. "I'm here to see Ethan Miller. I was told he's in ICU."

"Mr. Miller is only allowed one visitor at a time. I'm sorry, there is someone visiting him now. If you don't mind waiting until she leaves, you can go in."

She. Did the nurse say "she"?

I went and sat in a little waiting room down the hall. It had a few chairs up against the cold, bare walls, magazines that had been read numerous times, and a TV mounted on the wall. A news channel was on. I looked at the TV but had no idea what they were talking about, the volume was too low. The president was saying something about the Middle East. You would think that they would put on a channel that was a little less stressful, especially when family members are waiting to hear about someone in the ICU. I kept looking down the hall, waiting for the woman to leave one of the rooms. After an hour, a young woman stepped out of the room on the left and started walking toward the elevators. She was tall and thin. It wasn't until she reached the elevators that I noticed her face was badly bruised; she had a swollen, black eye. Her right forearm was also bruised. She had taken one hell of a beating. Obviously, she was the girl he had helped. She pushed the elevator button. I quickly rushed to the elevator so I could speak to her before the elevator reached the tenth floor. I put my hand on her arm; she turned in surprise.

"Excuse me, please. I am a friend of Ethan. Did you just come from his room?" She nodded. "I'm here to see him, but they told me he had another visitor and that I should wait. I'm sorry about what happened to you. How are you feeling?"

She nodded. "Okay, I guess."

I looked at her beautiful, battered face. "You're very lucky he was there to stop those animals."

She frowned. "I know, that's why I'm here. I was hoping he would be awake. I wanted so desperately to thank him. If it weren't for him, well, I just don't know. I could be dead. He's still unconscious, but the doctor is optimistic. I'll come back again tomorrow. Hopefully he'll be awake. I saw him sitting in the bar by himself having a drink, not speaking to anyone. The next thing I know, he's saving my life."

I had to get her name before she left. I had to say something. "Would you like to tell me your name? When he wakes up, I can tell him you were here. I'm sure he would be glad to know you're up to visiting him."

"My name is Darcy. How do you know Ethan?"

Luckily, the elevator had reached the tenth floor, and she stepped in. I put out my hand, and she took it. "Good luck to you, Darcy. I hope you feel better soon." She smiled and the elevator door closed.

I was extremely glad I didn't have to answer her question. You could see behind the bruises and black eye that she was a beautiful girl. Someone that attractive could catch the eye of the animals that attacked her. *Why would she walk alone that time of night?*

I walked down the hall to Ethan's room and looked in. His head was bandaged, and his eye was covered as well. Jake didn't say anything about his eye being injured. He was hooked up to monitors, but he seemed to be resting comfortably. I stood there looking at him with such a heavy heart, tears streaming down my cheeks. I whispered to that beautiful face, "Please wake up, Ethan. You need to wake up. It's Liz. Can you hear me?"

This man had no one—no family, wife, children, or girlfriend. How much more does one person deserve? I was just about to leave when I heard two voices talking to the nurse at the station. They were asking if Ethan had any visitors today.

She said, "The girl he had helped spent some time sitting in his room. But there was no response from Ethan. There was also another woman who waited awhile. Only one visitor at a time, you know. When the first woman left, the second woman spoke to her briefly by the elevator, and then she went down the hall to see Ethan. She looked very upset."

I listened carefully to what the nurse was telling them. One voice I totally didn't recognize, and *oh my god, the other voice was Jake. I didn't expect him to be at the hospital so early. He couldn't see me here.* Before they came to Ethan's room, I slipped out and went into the empty room next to Ethan's.

I stood behind the curtain. When their backs were to the door, as the doctor checked Ethan, I quickly slipped out of the room and gave the nurse a quick wave and smile. With any luck, the elevator would be here before she could call the doctor and Jake to tell them I was by the elevator. The down arrow lit up, and the doors opened. I stepped in, and the doors closed. I made it, thank *God.*

I went straight home and was sitting on the couch with a glass of wine when Jake came in the door. "Where were you all day, Emma? When I woke up, you weren't here. I couldn't imagine where you would have gone so early."

I just smiled and said, "I felt like taking a walk. I stopped in a couple of stores and considered going for a trim, but Sally was booked. So I just came home. My cell was dead. I forgot to charge it, so I couldn't call you. Sorry, I didn't mean to worry you." Where did you go, Jake, to the office or the hospital?"

He looked at me as if he wasn't sure he believed what I was telling him, and honestly, it was kind of a lame story, but I needed to see Ethan.

"I went to the VA to see Captain Miller. I'm relieved to report he has regained consciousness. Amazingly, a few minutes after the doctor and I walked into the room to check on him, he woke up. They're not sure what extent of the trauma is, but at least he's up. The nurse at the desk said he had two visitors today. One was the young attractive woman he had helped. She was pretty badly bruised. The other woman, the nurse said, was a friend who looked terribly upset and just wanted to see how Captain Miller was doing. She said we had just missed her. He had never mentioned any female friends in our sessions. I am kind of surprised. But there was still the number on the Macy's receipt. Maybe that was her?"

I could feel my hands start to sweat. So a few minutes after I left, Jake and the doctor walked in and Ethan came to. *Could it be he had recognized my voice and heard me say it was Liz? Could that have given him the will to wake up?*

"The doctors said they should know more by tomorrow. I'm going to go back in the morning. I want to see if I can help in any way. As his psychiatrist, I feel I should be there, it's my responsibility."

"Whatever you feel is best, Jake. I hope there is something you can do."

I truly hoped Jake could help.

Chapter 11

Now that Ethan was awake…

What if he remembered and told Jake he was having an affair? He didn't know my real name, and if he described me, I looked like a million other women in New York. Jake would never link the two.

I was still concerned about the police getting involved and finding my heart in the apartment. But that didn't seem to be happening yet. Jake's cell buzzed. It was Dr. Harris calling from the VA hospital; he wanted to give Jake an update on Ethan's condition. After talking to the doctor for a while, Jake hung up, feeling very disturbed.

"Apparently, Ethan doesn't remember the incident of helping the young woman. He has mild trauma to the brain; it's causing a disturbance in his memory."

"How much has he forgotten?" I asked.

"It's called post-traumatic amnesia. He can have loss of memory for the present time and an inability to recognize even the most familiar faces. He might have some confusion, agitation, and even some anxiety. Sometimes, a person has no recall of their day-to-day life or even past events. It can last for minutes or up to several months. The doctors can't be sure."

Dr. Harris asked Jake if he would be available to come to the VA and evaluate Ethan's condition since there might be episodes of agitation and anxiety. He planned to go over sometime this afternoon.

Maybe, Ethan won't remember being with me. Then it will all be in the past, and I'll go on with my life. Jake will never know. Ethan will go on being Jake's patient, and I'll know Ethan will be in good hands. I did want him to get the help he so badly needed. Now if only I could find a way to get my heart. Maybe, his neighbor, Suzanne, will get back to me soon. Maybe she won't get back to me at all. I told Jake it was being repaired. I should have just said I misplaced it somewhere in our apartment. I'm sure it will turn up. Who knew all this was going to get so complicated? I had no idea how I'm going to get through this.

At two, after lunch, Jake announced he was going to the hospital. I asked him if he wanted company, but I knew that the answer would be no. Of course, I was right. He said he should only be a couple of hours. He didn't want to overwhelm Ethan. This was the first time that Jake would be visiting him after he regained consciousness. He didn't want to pressure him with questions about what happened that night. Jake walked out the door. I pulled a book off the shelf in the living room, threw myself on my bed and opened the book. I tried to read but couldn't concentrate. I was too concerned with what Ethan might remember and say to Jake. *Ironically, the book I pulled off the shelf was about a cheating husband. How's that for a twist?* I put it down and laughed like a woman on the edge.

*****

When Jake got to the hospital, Ethan was no longer in the intensive care unit and had been moved to a regular room on the fifth floor. It was a shared room, but the other bed was empty. Jake was grateful for that. He could talk to Ethan with privacy and without interruption. However, Ethan didn't want to talk to Jake. He had no idea who Jake was.

Jake explained that he was Ethan's psychiatrist and had been treating him for PTSD. If Ethan needed someone to talk to, he would be more than willing to help him. Jake didn't want to press him; he left him alone and gave him time to think about it. He hoped when he revisited Ethan again, things would be different. As Jake was leaving the hospital, he met Dr. Harris coming down the hall. He told Jake that the young woman who was there the other day had come back to the hospital. Again, she wanted to try to thank Ethan for saving her life. Dr. Harris was checking Ethan's eye, which was injured by the blow to his face. The young woman walked into the room. Dr. Harris stayed; he wanted to see Ethan's reaction. Maybe seeing her would spark something in his memory. As she walked toward the bed, Ethan smiled and called her Liz. But when she was next to the bed, he didn't recognize her face. She tried to thank him, but he said he didn't remember the incident of helping her.

She was obviously upset at Ethan's condition, and his not remembering her only made her feel worse. Dr. Harris walked her from the room and explained that Ethan was suffering from a form of amnesia. Hopefully, his memory would come back soon. When it did, Dr. Harris would let her know. She could come back and try to visit again. There was nothing she could do, and it certainly wasn't her fault Ethan had come to her aid. He asked for her name and number so he would be able to call if there was a change in Ethan's condition. She gave the doctor her business card, shook his hand, and left in tears.

Dr. Harris wondered who Liz was and how they could find out more information about her. Maybe, he mentioned Liz to Jake. Jake told Dr. Harris that Ethan mostly talked about the military. He asked Jake if he could try to help Ethan remember her.

*****

Jake was home within the hour. He explained everything Dr. Harris had told him. The young woman had been at the hospital again. Ethan still could not remember her and called her by another name. I needed to hear what was happening with Ethan, no matter how upsetting it might be. Jake went on. Then he told me the name he called the young woman.

When I heard the name Liz, my whole body went numb. I looked at Jake, faking confusion. "So are you sure the girl Ethan helped wasn't Liz? Do you and Dr. Harris have any idea who this Liz might be?"

He poured himself a drink. "Not a clue. The name on the card she gave Dr. Harris was Darcy. Ethan did mention he met someone in passing at one of his sessions but never gave details, not even a name. Maybe that was Liz. He did say though that she was pretty special and I would probably like her." *Funny.*

My world was spinning out of control. I felt as if my life was coming to a crashing halt. If Ethan regained his memory and started talking about Liz, how long would it be before Jake finds out that I was Liz? Again, I prayed that Ethan's neighbor would call me so I could get the heart out of the apartment. That was the key to separating me from Liz.

Everything in the room was fading to black. Jake was still talking to me, but all I heard was muffled sounds. That was the last thing I remember. I woke up on the couch. Jake was standing over me, tapping my cheek and putting a damp towel on my head. "Emma, what the hell happened? Are you all right? One minute you're listening to me and the next you're as white as a ghost on the floor. What's wrong?"

I sat up and put my head back on the couch. "Honestly, I don't know. I haven't been feeling very well lately. Nauseous, dizzy, and a little light-headed. Maybe I'm coming down with something."

I'm coming down with a nervous breakdown. That's what I'm coming down with.

"I'll call the doctor, I promise, and make an appointment for a checkup." *What I didn't tell Jake was that the appointment I think I should make was with Dr. DiMario.* I should have gotten my period days ago, and nothing. I would be forty shortly; hopefully I was starting menopause, or maybe it was just stress. "I'll call in the morning."

Chapter 12

I stood in the shower, warm water cascading over my body. I had called Dr. DiMario's office for an appointment. I fully expected to be told to come in a couple of weeks since he had a very hectic schedule. Surprisingly enough, they said there was a cancellation and to come in this afternoon around one forty-five. I'm sure that my period was late due to all the stress I had been under these past few weeks. I should definitely get it checked in case something was wrong.

I stepped out of the shower and heard my cell going off. I threw a towel around me and ran to answer, but I had missed the call. It was Ethan's neighbor. I immediately called her back. "Hello, Suzanne, it's Liz. I'm sorry I missed your call. What's going on?" My nerves were getting the better of me.

She sounded rushed. "Two detectives were at the building last night asking questions about Ethan and the girl who was attacked. I told them Ethan was just a neighbor and I didn't know the girl at all. They didn't ask if he was seeing anyone. Maybe you should get in the apartment soon. You know, to get the "toiletries." I called the landlord this morning and told him my bathroom sink has been leaking the past few days. It was just an excuse to get the super here for you. I let the sink overflow just a little so the floor would be a little wet. He said he called the maintenance workers to come and do repair work on the top floor hallway. He might as well tell them to come today and check my sink as well. I told him about Ethan being in the hospital. He said he'll have the workers go in Ethan's too. The manager has the keys to all the apartments. He'll ask him to have a look around to make sure everything is still in order. I was thinking if you were available to come by, you can come up with some excuses to tell the workers to let you into the apartment. You can get what you had forgotten. They should be here around ten thirty. Can you make it?"

There was no doubt about it. "Of course I'll be there, Suzanne, thank you so much. You're a lifesaver. I owe you big time for this."

"I'm sorry, Liz. I'll be at work. And you don't owe me anything. Trust me, I get it, but you're going to have to pull the rest of this off on your own."

She hung up. I looked at the clock; it was nine fifteen. I needed to hurry, get dressed, and rush to Ethan's building before the maintenance men were done with their work. That would still give me plenty of time to get to Dr. DiMario's office by one for-ty-five. I arrived at the building just when the men were getting there.

I approached a middle-aged man getting out of a panel truck that said LoPorto Bros. Maintenance and Repairs on the side. The truck looked like it could use some maintenance of its own. He walked around to the back, opened the doors, and started taking out tools. I approached him nonchalantly and asked, "Are you Mr. LoPorto? I was told you would be here today. My friend, Ethan, who lives on the second floor in this building is in the hospital. He was attacked the other night. Would it be possible for you to let me in his apartment?"

He gave me a curious glance and then nodded in the affirmative. "I would like to pick up some things he needs. He would really appreciate it. Oh, thank you Mr. LoPorto, I won't be but five minutes."

He gave me a crooked smile, looked me up and down, and asked ever so curtly, "So tell me, sweetheart, what did you leave behind? A wedding ring, perhaps a pair of sexy lace panties?"

I thought I would die right there on the spot. Dirty old man. "Well, if you really must know, it was a sexy black teddy my other boyfriend gave me, and I'm supposed to see him tonight. He will definitely miss it. Happy now? Not that this is any of your business."

He shook his head as we climbed the stairs, and he opened the door to Ethan's apartment. There was still the faint smell of his cologne in the air. Just the scent and the memory of our lovemaking aroused me. *Emma, just get the heart and leave.*

The apartment was still very organized, nothing out of place. I walked over to the nightstand and looked for the heart, but it wasn't there. I looked under the nightstand; it wasn't there either. Then something shimmering on the bed pillow caught my eye. It was the heart. Ethan had placed my heart, ever so neatly, on the pillow next to his. *Why would he do that? Why would he leave it on his bed? It gave me such a strange feeling.* I picked up the heart, walked out, and closed the door behind me.

I yelled up to Mr. LoPorto, who was doing his repairs upstairs, "I'm done. My boyfriend will appreciate this. Thanks again."

I ran down the stoop and walked to my car a block away. The heart resting on the pillow had really unnerved me. *What was Ethan thinking? He was hurt on Thursday night. I wasn't due there till Saturday afternoon. It was so strange. Why leave it there two days? He could have moved it Thursday night but never got home. My mind just kept racing. What was he thinking? Why on the pillow?*

I got in the car and put the heart back around my neck. Now all I have to do is tell Jake I finally went to the jewelers and picked it up. Thank God that was done. I stopped at Starbucks and ordered a latte. I really shouldn't have caffeine, I'm nervous enough. I needed to head over to the doctor's office. I'm so sure it's stress.

I reached Dr. DiMario's office a little early. I've been coming to this office for so many years, and yet when I walked in today, I had an overwhelming feeling of anxiety. Maybe, it was remembering my previous miscarriages and the thought that I may be pregnant again. I felt as if I might burst into tears. *Compose yourself, Emma.* There were three quite pregnant women waiting to see him. I remembered those days so sadly. I would have had a fifteen-year-old by now if I hadn't lost the first child. He would be a high school student. I wondered what his interest would have been. Would it be psychology, like his dad, or would he have an interest in forensics, like me? Who knows; maybe a great detective like Grandpa? I still have my job at the library with the children and my volunteer work in pediatrics at the hospital. It's not the same as having your own child and watching them grow into an amazing person, but it's still very rewarding. I knew that I would be waiting a while. I picked up a magazine and started to read an article on how to improve your sex life.

Oh hell no! If you want to have great sex, sleep with Ethan Miller. That will do the trick. Then have tons of guilt and stress. I can definitely write my own how-to article on that subject. All these women sitting here with their big bellies must have been doing just fine in the sex department. When I finished the article, there was one woman left ahead of me. She noticed the article I was reading, looked at me, and smiled. Believe me, according to this article, I didn't need any self-help. I was doing just fine. *Maybe, it was too good.* I put the magazine down and waited. The nurse called me in. I was escorted to a room and given a gown.

"This isn't your routine checkup. What brought you in today, Mrs. Farrell?"

I told her that my period was a few days late and I fainted last night. I thought that I would just come in and check my blood pressure and run some blood tests.

"Well, Mrs. Farrell, did you do a home pregnancy test?"

Home pregnancy test? Why would I do a home pregnancy test? "Actually, I didn't, but I'm positive I'm not pregnant. We stopped trying years ago. Jake and I are very careful. We don't want the heartache of any more miscarriages. I've been under tremendous stress lately. I'm sure that's it."

She smiled and handed me a pregnancy test. "Humor me, Mrs. Farrell. Go in the bathroom and pee on the stick."

Can't you say urinate? I might as well get this over with and prove I'm not pregnant. Into the bathroom I went and *urinated* on the stick. I walked out of the bathroom and handed her the stick. I didn't even look at it, sure of the results.

She took the stick and smiled. "Congratulations, Mrs. Farrell, you are pregnant!"

"Are you sure? Let me see that thing. That can't be right." I grabbed the stick from her hand. Sure enough, there was a little plus sign on the stick.

"Mrs. Farrell, these things are 99 percent accurate. You're pregnant. Wait in room three and Dr. DiMario will be with you in a few minutes."

I thought of Ethan saying three was always his lucky number and his little marching marines making their way into Camp Uterus. Yes, Jake and I were careful most of the times, but then again, Ethan and I were another story. I'm going to be sick. I had sex with Jake and Ethan in the same weekend. How will I know who is the father? Did Jake use a condom on that night? Oh god, I didn't think so. I was still dazed from the night before. How could I let this happen to me and to Jake? Neither one of them used protection. Ethan must have thought that I was on the pill, and why not, a married woman at my age. I'm almost forty. What were the chances of getting pregnant? More and more women were getting pregnant in the forties. Jake used condoms at appropriate times. Being told a due date wouldn't help determine who the father might be.

Dr. DiMario came in the room. "I hear congratulations are in order, Emma."

I burst into tears.

"Emma, what's with the tears? I know you stopped trying to conceive a long time ago, but maybe this is your second chance. Sometimes, things happen for a reason. I'm sure Jake will be happy."

Then I really burst into tears.

"Why are *you* so upset?"

I just blurted out, "Doc, I don't even know if I should have this child. How can this happen so late in my life? I'm too old."

He just looked at me in surprise. "Emma, many women today are having children in the late thirties, early forties. It's not that unusual. In the meantime, let me do some blood work and check you out to be certain."

Dr. DiMario knew Jake and I had a good marriage for over fifteen years. He would have never suspected that there was another man who could possibly be the father of this child, and I wasn't about to tell him.

"Emma, nothing is etched in stone. Go home and think about what would be the right choice for you and, of course, Jake. You don't have to go through with this pregnancy if you don't want to, but I can't see any reason why you shouldn't."

He put his arm around my shoulder. "I would suggest, though, you really think long and hard before you make such a drastic decision. This is something you wanted so badly in the past. Decide what you should do with Jake. He is your husband and I know you two would be great parents."

Yes, Jake and I would make great parents, but what about Ethan?

Chapter 13

I walked through Central Park shrouded in depression. I couldn't go home. My mind was like a merry-go-round, with its colorful horses falling off their tracks, going in all different directions.

Keep the child, abort the child, tell Jake I'm pregnant, don't tell Jake. Tell him about Ethan. Don't tell him about Ethan. Go to the nearest bridge and jump off.

Jake should be home by now, and I just couldn't face him. The baby could be his, but how would I know for sure? I would need a DNA test. How could I do that without breaking his heart? Bring his DNA to a lab, take his toothbrush, a comb, more lying, and sneaking. I just couldn't cope with the lying anymore. I kept walking and walking. Finally, I sat on a bench and remembered the times Jake and I would sit here and he would listen to me talk about my love of forensics. The days were getting shorter now. The air was getting cooler. I had to go home and face what was in store for me. By the time I opened my front door, the apartment was covered in darkness.

Jake wasn't home yet. Where could he be?

I didn't turn on the lights and went straight to the sofa and sat down. I must have fallen asleep. I woke up to Jake tapping me on the shoulder. "Kid, are you okay? What did the doctor say?"

"Oh, Jake, what time is it? I must have passed out."

"Emma, what *did* the doctor say? Why did you faint last night?"

I couldn't get the words out. "He did some blood work. He'll get back to me with the results in a couple of days. He said I should be fine. I'm just a little tired. I might be a little anemic. How come you're getting home so late? Jake, is everything okay?"

"I was at the hospital. Ethan Miller is starting to get his memory back, not totally, but bits and pieces. He has flashes of helping the girl and the fight. He keeps saying something about a girl named Liz, but he doesn't remember who she is. Her name keeps popping up in his head. He can't remember many specifics about her, just that he cared for her. He does recall something about an elevator and a piece of jewelry. I'll see him again tomorrow. Maybe I can get him to recall something else. She might be very important to him, and she doesn't even know that he's in the hospital."

Oh, believe me she knows he's in the hospital. She knows the whole story!

"The bad news is he lost partial vision in his injured eye. But he seems to be coping with that rather well, so far. He's been through so much already. I don't know where he gets his strength."

Let's see how much more pain can we add to this drama. I'm done, I'm going to bed.

"Jake, I'm going to bed. I'm so tired. It was a long day; are you coming?"

"I'll be in soon. Good night, Kid."

I went into the bathroom, rinsed my face and brushed my teeth, put on my nightgown, and slid into bed. I laid there like a rag doll staring at the ceiling.

How much more can Jake get Ethan to remember? Jake came in a few minutes later, got in bed and rested his hand on my stomach. It was as if he had a premonition of what was happening inside my body.

"I love you, Kid, you know that, don't you?"

"Yes, Jake, I do. I love you too."

The week went along without incident. Jake continued to visit Ethan after his office appointments. Ethan remembered nothing else. I worked at the library and volunteered at the children's hospital. I got a phone call from Dr. DiMario. He informed me that I was in excellent health, and yes, I was going to be a mother.

Now, let's just figure out who the father might be.

He asked me if I had talked to Jake and made any decisions. I said I needed some more time. I couldn't think straight. I couldn't tell Jake yet. He suggested I should tell him soon. Maybe, tonight should be the night. A romantic dinner, quiet, just the two of us, and I'll give him the news. We will decide what to do together. I will just resign myself to the fact that this child is ours and ours alone. He didn't need to know anything different.

I was walking back from the market when my cell rang. It was Jake. Good. I'll tell him about the dinner and ask what time I should have it ready.

"Hi, Jake, I'm glad you called. What time do you think you'll be home for dinner tonight?"

"I'm sorry, Em, I just got off the phone with Dr. Harris. They want to discharge Ethan Miller today. There is no reason to keep him in the hospital. Physically, he's doing much better, but he still needs therapy to help with the amnesia. That's where I come in. Dr. Harris was wondering if I could help him get home tonight, see if he recognizes his apartment, and maybe, it will help him bring back some memories. There might be a picture of our mystery lady *Liz*."

Thank God I was able to get into the apartment and retrieve my heart. I certainly know there was no picture of me anywhere in the apartment. We could talk when Jake gets home.

"Jake, it's not a problem. I'll make dinner, and we can eat when you get home. How's that sound?"

"Good to me. See you later, love you."

"I love you too."

Dinner was just about done. I didn't cook anything too fancy, just spaghetti and meatballs, garlic bread, and bottles of red and white wine. I shouldn't drink, but one glass won't hurt. I knew I'd need it. I heard the front door open.

"Jake, that was fast. I didn't think you would be home for a while. Dinner will be ready soon."

I started walking into the foyer to kiss him hello, and I froze in my tracks. Standing next to Jake was Ethan, with a white bandage over his eye.

"Emma, this is Capt. Ethan Miller, I hope you don't mind I brought a guest home for dinner. Ethan, this is my wife, Emma."

He put out his hand, and I shook it.

"Mrs. Farrell, I hope this isn't too much of an imposition. I told Doc here women don't like to be surprised with a dinner guest, but he insisted."

I could feel my heart pounding in my chest. Seeing the two of them standing side by side was way too much for me to handle. I could hardly breathe.

"Call me Emma, please, and it's no problem at all."

Jake interrupted, *thank God*, "I told Ethan I couldn't bring him home to an empty apartment without feeding him a nice home-cooked meal first. You said you were making dinner anyway. He'll need to get used to things all over again, and I'm sure cooking isn't the first thing on your mind, right, Ethan?"

Ethan just nodded. We went into the living room; *the potential fathers of my baby standing side by side.* Jake and I sat on the sofa, Ethan sat in the chair across from us.

"Emma, that's quite a beautiful heart you have." He kept staring at it.

"E. F. for Emma Farrell, a lovely heart for a lovely lady."

Did he remember?

"Thank you, Ethan. It was an anniversary gift from Jake. He has wonderful taste." I put my hand over the heart as if I was trying to hide it. I could feel my face start to flush.

Ethan smiled. "Yes, he most certainly does."

This was making my body numb. I excused myself and went into the kitchen and drank a cold glass of water, my hands trembling. I composed myself and called out, "Well, dinner is ready. Shall we eat?"

We walked to the dinner table. I put out another place setting. Ethan sat while Jake and I walked into the kitchen to get the food and wine. Jake opened the wine and placed it on the table.

"Ethan, would you mind pouring while I help Emma with the food?" Ethan stood and picked up the bottle of red. He poured a glass for himself and Jake. But then as if it was a natural thing to him, he picked up the white and poured it in my glass.

"Good choice, Ethan, how did you guess?" Jake's voice was almost suspicious.

"I don't know, just lucky, I guess. I find in my experience with women that they usually drink white. Oh, look, Doc, I actually remembered something."

I knew I shouldn't drink it, but if I didn't Jake would wonder why.

During dinner, I could barely touch my food. I kept my gaze focused on Jake, and every so often, I would glance over at Ethan. Each time I looked at that face, I remembered our intense lovemaking and the passion he aroused in me; how my body had responded to his touch as if our bodies were molded so perfectly to each other. And now I sit here with these two men. One I loved for so many years, the other I barely know and yet stirs so much in me. Either one could be the father of the child I'm carrying. I could barely say a word.

Jake discussed Ethan's amnesia with him. He had some memories of helping the young woman, this he had previously discussed with Jake. But the weeks before were a blur. He remembered an elevator and the name Liz which kept running through his mind. He didn't know why. Jake took another sip of wine and put the glass down. "We'll work on that, Ethan, and we'll find her."

I stood up. "Will you excuse me for a minute, please?" I went in the bathroom and became ill. I didn't know how much more of this I could handle, mentally or physically.

When I returned, Jake looked at his watch. "Well, Ethan, I guess it's time to get you home." He stood up, and I was grateful he wasn't staying longer.

"Yep, it's getting late. Let's see how much of my place can bring back some sordid memories." He grinned. "And I want to thank you, Emma, for a delicious dinner."

They started walking toward the door. I walked along beside them. "Ethan, I hope everything works out for you. I really do."

"Thank you again." He leaned forward and kissed my cheek.

I held my breath. Jake seemed unfazed by this little show of affection. As they headed for the elevator, I heard a clap of thunder and rain tapping against the windows. I called to Jake, "Wait, it's starting to rain. Let me get you two an umbrella." I rushed to the elevator and handed it to Jake.

As the elevator closed, Ethan looked directly into my eyes.

Something in his memory clicked. Was it me by the elevator or when I was at his apartment making love during the thunderstorm? I could see it in his eyes, he remembered something.

Would he say something to Jake?

Lovely wife you have, Doc, great in bed too.

Chapter 14

Jake had come back from Ethan's apartment. I finished cleaning up dinner and was sitting on the sofa flipping channels. I wasn't watching anything in particular. Jake sat next to me.

"Well, that was a very awkward dinner, I must say."

I turned and looked at him with a curious expression on my face. "Really, Jake, how so?"

Where was this conversation going?

"Well, Emma, I could see you were very uncomfortable, and Ethan couldn't take his eyes off of you. It was as if he had you in the recesses of his mind, trying to remember something about you, where he might have seen you or spoken to you. I'm a psychiatrist, Em, it's my job to read people, and I think I read you two pretty well. You could have cut the tension with a knife." He paused and began again.

"And you know a funny thing happened when we arrived at Ethan's apartment. His downstairs neighbor, a cute little blonde, came out of her apartment. She asked Ethan if his friend was able to get in his apartment and pick up what she had left behind. She couldn't have known Ethan had amnesia, who would have told her? She suspected it was probably an earring or a piece of jewelry. No woman would be that concerned over a panty; she laughed about it.

"Ethan couldn't recall who she might have been talking about or anyone leaving something of value in his apartment. She also told Ethan that she said her name was Liz, a pretty woman around mid-to-late thirties. You know, the classy type. He still had no recollection of who she might be, but he did remember the name Liz. If he did remember who she was, he certainly did not let on. I personally wonder who she is and what her connection to Ethan was. What could she have possibly left behind? Maybe it was her wedding band. Probably married to some poor rich sucker." He smirked.

Was Ethan just pretending not to remember?

"Jake, for God's sake, what are you talking about? Your imagination is getting the best of you. Maybe it was some woman he slept with a few times and was a little careless with her belongings. As far as I'm concerned, I was uncomfortable, yes. Was dinner awkward? Yes. I was just a little upset. I didn't expect an unannounced guest for dinner, and by the way, thank you for that, I really appreciated it. You also know I haven't been feeling that great. Maybe I just wanted a nice, relaxing evening with my husband. To be quite honest, Jake, I don't like being accused of whatever you're insinuating or, for that matter, what you thought Ethan might have been thinking about me. Maybe he just thought I was attractive or even hot for that matter. How would any of that be my fault? And if you want to know the truth, I think he is as hot as hell. I would love to screw his brains out. Any woman would. Is that what you want to hear? I'm definitely not having this ridiculous conversation with you. I'm going to bed. You should be nice and comfortable out here on the sofa."

I walked into the bedroom and slammed the door. I knew I was overreacting, mostly because Jake was absolutely right and my own guilt was getting the better of me. He was the one who brought Ethan home for dinner. I was hoping Ethan would have *never* remembered me. A few minutes later, Jake opened the door to the bedroom.

"Emma, one more question. When were you going to tell me you're pregnant? Nice try just sipping your wine."

I was stunned. "What? How do you know, Jake?"

He sat on the foot of the bed. "I called Dr. DiMario's office and asked to speak to him. I was very concerned after you fainted the other night. He told me congratulations, Emma. He thought you must have told me by now."

"Jake, he had no right to say anything to you, and you had no right to call his office. What happened to doctor/patient confidentiality? Does that only apply to you and your patients?" I jumped off the bed and walked toward the bathroom.

"Emma, I'm your husband. He knows us for years. I'm sure he felt he wasn't doing anything wrong."

Tears began to fill my eyes. "If you must know, Jake, I was going to tell you tonight over dinner. But then you brought home our very sexy dinner guest, you know the one you think I want to screw and all this mayhem started. Thank you again for ruining what could have been a wonderful evening. Please, get out of the bedroom, Jake, I'm tired. The baby and I would like to get some rest."

When Jake came into the kitchen the following morning, I was standing at the stove making scrambled eggs and bacon. I was still very much annoyed with him for last night. I thought I would play the dutiful wife and make some breakfast. I sat at the table with him, all smiles and ate my eggs. He started to apologize. I put my hand up to stop him.

"Just let it go, Jake. I don't want to discuss it anymore." *Partially because of my own guilt.*

He had no idea that when he left for the office after breakfast, I was leaving for the Hamptons. I needed to get out of the city for a while and away from Jake and Ethan.

"What about the baby, Emma? What do you want to do about the baby?" He looked worried.

"The baby and I are just fine, no need to concern yourself."

He left the table, put his plate in the sink, and headed for the door. "Kid," he started again, but I cut him short.

"Jake, I'm not a kid anymore. Have a good day." The door closed.

I called my dad and told him I was going to the Hamptons for a few days. I would talk to him during the week. I'll be fine and not to worry. Next, I called the library. I told the head librarian that I was not feeling well and I needed some time off. She was very understanding. She told me to rest up and she would be glad to see me when I got back to the library.

Next, Jake. I'll leave him a note. I didn't want to talk to him and have him try to convince me not to go until we spoke in person. I won't answer my phone if his number comes up. I went to the bedroom and packed a small bag. Before I left, I wrote the note to Jake and put it on the dining room table.

I stared at it for a moment thinking, *Do I really want to do this? Yes, I do.* I turned and walked out the door.

> *Jake,*
>
> *I've gone to the Hamptons for a few days. I need some alone time. I have a lot of thinking to do. I have to make some very important decisions. They are mine and mine alone to make. I wanted you to be part of that decision-making process, but after last night, I'm not sure what I want to do. Please don't contact me.*
>
> *Don't call or come out. I really hope you will respect my wishes.*
>
> *Emma*

Chapter 15

I pulled into the cottage driveway around noon. I hadn't called the housekeeper to straighten up. I really didn't care about the condition of the house right now.

The last time I was here, Jake and I had an enjoyable weekend, but guilt overshadowed my thoughts. I remembered being so physically uncomfortable making love to Jake from the intense sex I had with Ethan the night before. When could I have conceived the baby; was it with Jake or with Ethan? This had turned into such a nightmare. It's entirely my fault, and yet, I am so angry with Jake for being so suspicious. How can I be so unreasonable? After all, he was right in his suspicions. I'm just angry with myself for allowing all this to happen.

I walked into the house that was filled with so many special memories. Those memories included Jake. I went upstairs and opened the door to the little storage room. The room Jake and I had planned to turn into a nursery one day. Maybe, that day could be now. I walked around the room, thinking of the baby I was carrying. I was so confused. I needed to think. I went into our bedroom and rested on the bed. The bed Jake and I had made love on so many times. I put my hand on Jake's pillow. My heart was aching.

It was late in the afternoon; I was still curled up on the bed. The sun was setting, leaving the house with such morose feeling. Jake wasn't there next to me. He wasn't there to sit on the porch swing and talk with me.

He wasn't here to walk on the beach holding my hand. I needed this time alone. I needed to see what it would feel like without Jake by my side. It's like that old saying, *"You don't know what you have, till it's gone."*

But he wasn't gone yet.

Jake had bought me this house so long ago after my miscarriages to help me heal emotionally and become whole. Was that the fate that awaits this little peanut, resting in my body, another miscarriage?

Please, dear God, don't let that happen again. Could this house help me? I put my hand on my stomach and spoke to the baby, "I might not be sure who your dad is, Peanut, and I am so sorry for that, but I will try to be the best mom I can be."

First decision made: I'm keeping *my* baby. As if on cue, my stomach began to rumble.

"Are you hungry, Peanut? Me too. There's nothing in the house to eat. Let's go into town and pick up some food. What do you say? Good, I'm glad you agree." I drove down the road to the little grocery store. I picked out some pregnancy friendly foods and went back to the house. I made myself a cheese sandwich and poured a glass of milk. I peeled a banana for dessert. *No white wine for you, Peanut.* "How's that, feel better? Good."

Jake didn't call. He's either respecting my wishes or he hasn't gotten home from the office yet and read my note. Another decision that needed to be made. Obviously, Jake was concerned about me and the baby last night. He would want this child. Do I tell Jake that he might not be the father of this baby? Honesty is always the best policy, but what if honesty destroys our marriage? I didn't want to lose him. Jake would be an amazing father; this I truly believe.

Do I tell Ethan he might be the father? Every man has the right to know when he was about to become a father, but what could he possibly offer this child? That's not to say he wouldn't be a good parent; his life has just been so chaotic. Would he be stable enough to be a father? He had told me once that he wouldn't want to marry or leave a girlfriend with his child if he was killed overseas. But he's home now. Does that still hold true? He was under so much stress from his time in the military. Could he cope with being a father, and would we be able to stay away from each other co-parenting? Does a child need to grow up with that in its life? Ethan was just someone I found extremely attractive. I let my desires overtake my common sense. I hardly knew this man. But the passion he aroused in me ran very deep. This was no longer *harmless*.

This was not harmless at all. It never was.

The phone rang, and I jumped up. It was my dad, of course. "Just checking in, Emma." My dad, ever the worrier. "Emma, what's going on? This isn't like you."

"I'm fine, Dad. I'll talk to you during the week." I didn't want to get into a long conversation with him right now.

Being in the cottage alone was surprisingly peaceful once I got used to it. I would talk to my little Peanut and ask him or her what should Mommy do. I would imagine the answers. We would watch TV, and every once in a while, I would read from anything I could find so the baby would get to know my voice.

My favorite part of the day would be sunset, sitting on the porch swing listening to music, watching the waves, and rocking back and forth. In the mornings, I would go to the little room and sit in an old rocking chair, which was left in the house when we bought it. I would get an idea on how I would like to decorate the room, whether it would be a boy or a girl.

"This is going to be your room, my little Peanut."

I liked nautical for a boy or princess for a girl. Jake should be here to help me pick. The loneliest part of the day was at night when I would go to bed. Jake was not beside me to wrap his arms around me. I would picture his face lying on his pillow, smiling at me, telling me he loved me. It would take me quite a while to fall asleep. He didn't call or text, and I'm sure he must have read my letter by now. It has been three days. Maybe, he needed time to think as well.

I had come to the decision that I want to keep my baby and I wanted to be with Jake. But I needed to know for sure who the father is. I could do the DNA test without him knowing, but what if it comes back that Ethan is the father? How could I tell him and break his heart? How would Jake react to such information? I'm sure he would be utterly destroyed. So would I. That was not something I could keep to myself. I would not be able to live with such a lie. Jake would need to know. Every time I looked at my Peanut's little face, whose face would I see?

They both have beautiful blue eyes. What do you think, Peanut, who will you look like? Help me. What should Mommy do?

Chapter 16

It was the morning of the fourth day. I was in the kitchen making myself breakfast when I heard a car pull into the driveway. Was it Jake? Did he drive out to talk? I went to the front door and opened it, with such excitement. But it wasn't Jake's Mercedes. Nobody else knew I was here. Who could it be? I didn't recognize the car. I stood by the front door and watched the driver's side door open. I didn't know what to expect, and I was getting very anxious.

He was looking as amazing as ever. *Emma, stop. How did he know where I was? Why was he here? Was I right when I thought he recognized me the night he came to dinner? He must have.*

"Ethan, what are you doing here? How did you know where to find me? Please, you can't be here. Go home, Ethan. You can't be here." I couldn't stop ranting. "Please, I just want to be left alone." *How did you know where to look?* I asked the same questions over and over.

"Oh, Emma or Liz, whatever you're calling yourself these days, calm down. It wasn't very hard to find you, not at all. You see, I had an appointment with Dr. Farrell—you know, Jake, your husband. I asked him how his lovely wife was doing, but of course, I knew you were just fine. He said you took a few days in the Hamptons. You needed a little quiet time and some rest. I understand congratulations are in order. You're pregnant. I am very happy for you. That's when I decided to come out and see you. I remembered you saying you had a cottage in Southampton. You told me about it when I called you after our first night together. You pretended I was your dad, remember? I asked around town, people here are so friendly. I said I was a friend of the Farrells. I was visiting and misplaced the address. The sweet teenager, pretty little thing, in the grocery store down the road was more than glad to help me. I guess I kind of have that effect on women. Don't you think so, Liz?"

"Ethan, please, go home. Don't do this." Tears filled my eyes.

"Don't do what, Emma Farrell, with your pretty little rose-gold heart? Ask you if I'm going to be a father? I know we were only together a couple of times, and boy, was it great, wasn't it, Liz? You seemed to enjoy it. But you know what they say, it only takes once. I mean I wouldn't want you to get pregnant and not take care of my responsibilities."

"Ethan, please, you're not the father. Jake is the father. Why would you even think it was yours? Stop it."

"Well, let's see, Emma. You've been married to Jake, for what, at least fifteen years now, and no babies. You've been with me a few times, and what do you know, a baby."

I couldn't believe the words that were coming out of his mouth. "Jake and I stopped trying years ago. It just wasn't meant to be for us."

"Oh, so now it was meant for you? How convenient."

"Ethan, why are you being so cruel and hurtful? What do you hope to accomplish?"

We were still standing on the porch. Ethan went and sat on the swing.

I pictured him sitting there once before, but he didn't belong there now.

"Ethan, can we please have this conversation inside?" We walked into the kitchen.

"So this is your little cottage. It's really nice. I can see why you like it here. I can grow to like it here myself." He looked at me with such a blank expression on his face.

"Emma, you're asking me why I am being so hurtful. Well, I can come up with a few reasons. Where do I start then? Let me ask you a few questions. Why are you such a liar? Why did you come home with me that Friday night? Why did you come back to me that rainy day? You love your husband, that's so obvious now. So what was it? You just wanted great sex, someone different than your genius husband? I looked like just the guy who could give you what you needed? What's the matter? Three isn't Jake's lucky number? Is he getting too old? You wanted me from the moment you bumped into me getting out of the elevator. I could have seen it in your eyes. You say you want to be with Jake. You want to believe Jake is the father of your baby. Fine. Be with Jake, but you're not going to get over me that easy. Every time you get in that elevator, you'll think of me. When you walk down the street, you're going to look for my face. Every time it rains or you hear a clap of thunder, you're going to think of that afternoon you came to my apartment, and I stripped you out of your soaking, wet clothes. You'll see my face when you're screwing Jake. You'll be looking into my eyes, not his. The thoughts of our lovemaking will keep you awake at night. I thought maybe you could have fallen in love with me. We were good together, Emma. For that short time, we were so good. It could have gone on. I knew you were married, but I didn't think it meant anything to you. You came home with me so easily. You made me feel like you really wanted me. Why would I think you love your husband?"

I just stood there. *He was right. It was beyond amazing. Maybe another time, maybe another place, it would have worked, but I was not willing to give up the life I had with Jake. I did use him, and he didn't deserve it, just liked I had lied to Jake. He didn't deserve it either. I started out thinking this was all harmless. I was so very wrong.*

"Ethan, I'm sorry, I really am. What I did was horribly wrong, I know that. I don't blame you, not for one minute. I can't say, in all honesty, Jake is the father. I really can't be sure, but that's where the baby and I belong, with Jake. You said you didn't want a wife or children. If something happens to you over-seas, you didn't want to leave them behind. I believed that, Ethan. I didn't think you wanted a commit-ment. And, yes, I was very attracted to you, so much so that I couldn't stop thinking about you or wanting you so badly it hurt. We were good together. We just don't belong together, but what I was doing hurt Jake as well. Please, just let it go."

His face looked so painful. I needed to convince him that it would be better for all involved if we just moved on. But I had one question that needed to be asked before I made him leave. It would haunt me forever if I never found out. "Ethan, why did I find my heart on the pillow next to yours and not on the nightstand like you said it would be when I went to your apartment to get it?"

He looked surprised at the question. "Why does it matter now? Do you really care, Emma?"

"Ethan, I need to know."

He looked into my eyes. "Because I needed you next to me, and that's all I had of you. I can still see it hanging from your neck when we made love."

I could feel my heart shattering into broken bits of glass. I couldn't believe his sad and lonely admis-sion. "I did really want you, Emma, for that short time, more than you would care to believe."

I didn't want to go on with this conversation.

"Emma, Jake doesn't know that the baby might be mine, does he?" He turned and stared out the kitchen window.

"No, Ethan, he doesn't. I'm not ready to tell him, not yet. Can you understand that?"

"No, I don't. Understand what? What was I, a harmless fantasy? A moment of weakness, I see. I'm glad I could fulfill your fantasy. I'm very happy to oblige. I guess you're not ready to tell Jake about your harmless fantasy either."

"No, Ethan, I'm not. Although I think he might have some idea." My voice was barely a whisper.

He started walking toward the door but stopped and then suddenly turned. It was as if he had to get these last few words out before he left. He had to drive the nail into my flesh one more time no matter how painful.

"I guess his arms hold you better than my arms held you and his kisses are better than my kisses. You don't want me to touch your body, let me kiss you, or fuck you anymore. I get it. The harmless fantasy is over. Unfortunately, it wasn't harmless to me. I'm glad I served my purpose. Good luck with the baby. I hope it works out the way you want it. But I'll always think he's mine and that he's out there happy and growing with his mother and a man who might not be his father."

He walked toward me, put his hand on my stomach as if he was caressing his child. He was saying goodbye. I was going to stop him, but I just didn't have the heart to do it. Tears were streaming down my cheeks. He gave me a gentle kiss on the lips, rested his chin on my forehead for a moment, and whispered, "Goodbye, Liz."

I could smell the faint scent of his cologne that I loved so much. I held my breath as he walked toward the car. He turned and looked at me, got in the car, and drove away.

He was gone.

I sat on the swing and sobbed. My mind drifted back to the day I bumped into him in the elevator. *Was it only a few months ago? It seemed like forever. I remembered how I felt when I saw that amazing man. The effect he had on me. Not being able to get him out of my mind. Walking through Macy's like a schoolgirl smelling his cologne on my arm. Seeing him standing there on the train platform, knowing he was coming to meet me on the promenade.*

Could I even look at the skyline again without thinking of him? How he so gently slipped me out of my wet clothes, making love to him on that rainy afternoon. How I felt looking at him lying in the hospital bed, praying for him to live. The scar on his body that showed how much physical pain he must have gone through. The mental scars he must carry in his mind. And now I only contributed to that scar.

Ethan thinking about a child that he might have created out there in the world, not knowing if he was the true father. How will he handle that not knowing? He was right. I could have fallen in love with him another time and another place. I won't get over him. I will look for his face in the crowds, and I will be disappointed when I don't see it.

I could have fallen in love with him so easily.

Chapter 17

And now here I am, staring out the window in the living room, watching the wind blowing through the leaves with all the strength it could muster. This house was once filled with happiness and love. Now it is dark, eerily so. And it is my fault. I know that now, and I couldn't forgive myself. Will he be able to forgive me? I think not. I couldn't even begin to ask for his forgiveness. I didn't deserve it.

This was the day I feared would come. The day I had dreaded for months. If only I could have stopped myself. Now it was here. How can I explain to a man who has loved me for so many years, a man that has given me such a good life? He has always been truthful and loyal. I hated myself, and I wouldn't blame him if he hated me too. I kept staring out the window, watching, looking down the dark lonely road, waiting for his Mercedes to pull into the driveway, unsuspecting of what he was about to hear...

I called Jake and asked him to come out to the cottage. It was time for us to have a very serious conversation.

He said he would be out after his last appointment, and he definitely agreed we needed to talk. How will I begin? There will be no more lies or false truths. I will bare my soul and ask for forgiveness. I will beg for forgiveness. The day seemed to drag, minutes like hours. Finally, I saw the headlights come down the dark road and turn into the driveway. I held my breath and put my hand on my stomach.

Here we go, Peanut. Mommy will have to deal with the consequences no matter what they might be, but I have you, I will always have you.

I went and sat in the living room, one lamp on. I could only speak to him in a cloud of darkness; I need to shroud my guilt. I heard his keys in the front door. He walked into the house. I could hear the sound of his footsteps in the hall. I felt as if he was walking in slow motion.

"Emma, I'm here. Where are you, Kid? How are you and the baby feeling?"

I couldn't call out to him; I was frozen with the terrible feeling of dread. He came into the living room and saw me in the chair.

"I missed you, Jake. We're both doing fine." I stood up and gave him a small kiss on his cheek. I went back to the chair and sat down. This could be the beginning of the end. I wanted it to be a new beginning for the three of us.

"Jake, I need to tell you so much. I don't know where to begin. I guess the beginning is always the best place. Before I start, please know that it was never my intention for things to get this out of control." He was going to say something, but I stopped him. "Please let me speak. I need to say what has to be said. Nor did I ever want to lie or hurt you in any way. I love you more than I can say."

"Emma, you don't need to do this. Anything you have to say will not make me love you any less. Nothing can be that bad. You're giving me a great gift. What can be more important to me than that? We never thought we would see this day. I knew you needed time to wrap your head around being pregnant again, and I left you alone. I respected your wishes, but I'm here now, and that's what is important to me. I want this child, Emma. I want us to be a family. And I'm sorry I made such foolish accusations about you and Ethan that night after dinner. I don't know what I was thinking. Maybe, I was just jealous of the way he kept staring at you. I should have known better."

"No, Jake, *I* should have known better. You weren't being so foolish. Please, stop. You don't understand…"

And I began trembling as I started my story from the moment I bumped into Ethan in the elevator to his visit here yesterday at the cottage. Jake said nothing. It was as if he had been shot through the heart. He sat with his elbows on his knees and hands folded together as if he was praying, *Please don't let this story be true.*

I left nothing out, except the very intimate details. I had to tell him everything. I couldn't live with myself if I didn't. When I was done, he said nothing; he just stared at the floor. Then he began to speak in a low, defeated voice.

"Emma, I love you and the child you're carrying, but let's just put that on the side for now. So let me see if I fully understand what you're telling me. When Ethan lost his memory, you were hoping he wouldn't remember you and I would never have known about the affair. You would have just gone on with our lives as if nothing had happened. And now you feel the need to be completely open and honest, you had a change of heart. How kind of you to be so considerate of me."

I could hear the sarcasm in his voice. I just let him talk. I wouldn't dare interrupt.

"But then I brought him home to dinner, and he started to remember you and, for lack of better words, *being with you*. That's why he was staring at you all through dinner. He started to recognize you and your heart. Did you wear it while you were screwing him? Of course you did. Is that where you left it while you told me it was supposed to be in the shop getting repaired? Oh, and let us not forget his pretty little neighbor who asked if his friend retrieved what she had left behind. You know, the pretty, *classy* lady. She was talking about you. Careless, Kid, really. I was right, and you made me feel like I was imagining it. Emma, you were making a fool out of me, and you were playing the poor little accused wife. I said I could have read you two like a book. I was right all along. He must have had some great memories of you, Kid. You thought your actions would have been *harmless,* I would have never known. Tell me, Emma, harmless for whom: you, me, Ethan? Please, Emma, tell me who were you trying to spare from your little indiscretion."

I started to say something, but Jake shook his head to stop me.

"How did you live with yourself while you were playing the dutiful little wife? Oh, and let us not forget that Ethan may possibly be the father of the baby." Tears filled his eyes.

"You slept with both of us one right after the other, giving you reason to doubt who the father might be. How can you screw Ethan one night and the next night lie in my arms and tell me you love me? I had no idea you were such a coldhearted bitch. When did this happen to you? When did you turn into such a slut?"

I knew this was a tremendous amount of hurt and anger talking, and who could blame him? Did I truly expect him to say "No problem, Kid? Forget it, let's live happily ever after. We can even make Ethan the godfather"?

He continued, "And Ethan, who does he think the father is? The big handsome manly marine. I'm sure he thinks it's his. You know the marines, get the job done. *Semper fi.* Well, I guess he can't discuss it with his psychiatrist now, can he? That would really be a conflict of interest, wouldn't you say so, Emma?" He stopped talking for a minute just looking at me. "Do you love him?" His eyes were sharp as a knife.

"I do have feelings for him, yes, but not the kind of love I have for you. I feel sorry for him. He is such a lost soul. What I did to both of you was terribly wrong. He didn't deserve what I did to him either. Jake, he didn't know I was your wife, not until he came home with you for dinner. I'm sure he would have never been with me if he knew."

"Yea, Em, but you see, the problem is *you* knew. That's the part that hurts the most. You knew you were my wife. How could you have forgotten that by just bumping into someone you thought would be fun to fuck? How could you have forgotten fifteen years of a good marriage?"

I whispered under my breath, "I never did forget."

"Coming to the hospital, saying you were concerned for me, seeing if I wanted to go get something to eat, all the while you were there to see how Ethan was doing. God, Emma, what the hell happened to you?"

"I love you, Jake, and he knows that. I told him the baby and I belong with you. He's gone, please, Jake."

He stood up and walked onto the porch. I wanted so much to run after him and beg him to stay, but I thought it best to leave him alone. He sat on the swing, slowly rocking back and forth, thinking, brushing tears from his eyes.

I sat in the chair again, waiting for him to come back into the house. Suddenly, I heard the car door slam shut and the engine start. I ran to the porch and watched his car drive away down the road. I could understand his pain and disappointment in me.

I was disgusted with myself.

He's a beautiful, compassionate man, and I could only pray that his love and soul will come back.

I will give him time…

We will give him time, Peanut.

Chapter 18

I gave birth to a beautiful baby girl on a bright, sunny morning. She had soft, wispy brown hair and the usual blue eyes most babies are born with. I knew someday they would change to the piercing blue eyes of her dad.

Ethan tried to contact me numerous times, but I never returned his calls. Jake referred him to another psychiatrist; of course, this was for the best. Jake couldn't bear to look at him, let alone treat him. They could never be in the same room again.

Jake and I separated; I moved into the cottage. After all, it was mine. It reminded me of when our lives were so good. I turned Jake's office into a beautiful princess nursery, waiting for my little Peanut's arrival. I left the small room for storage. It was filled with my belongings from the apartment in Manhattan. Jake was much too hurt to forgive me at this point, and the thoughts of not knowing if he was the father was way too much for him to live with. Dad would come out and stay with me every so often, and it was nice to have the company. He couldn't understand how

I allowed all this to happen, but he loved and sup-ported me with his whole heart and looked forward to being a grandpa.

About a month before I was due, I gave my father a piece of paper with two phone numbers. One was Jake's and the other was Ethan's. I told him when I was in labor to call them both. He was to tell each of them that I was in the hospital but I did not want them to come. I could do this on my own. He followed my wishes. He was short with them, not giving either of them any satisfaction. I could do a DNA test, but it didn't matter to me now. She was mine and mine alone. I did feel, however, they had the right to know that the baby had been born, whether they wanted her or not. I wanted to see who cared enough to ignore my wishes and come see the baby.

My little Peanut was rooming in with me at the hospital, but the nurses would take her to the nursery for her daily bath and to be weighed. She was doing just fine. So was I. I would sometimes take a little nap while she was in the nursery. Today, I didn't feel like sleeping.

The nurse came to my room. "Mrs. Farrell, someone left this little gift at the nurse's station for you. I asked if he wanted to deliver it himself, but he said it was better if I brought it in. He didn't want to disturb you. Nice-looking man, beautiful blue eyes." There in the nurse's hands was a cute little teddy bear dressed in camo fatigues, with a big pink bow. She handed it to me. I held it for a moment and then placed it next to my pillow on the bed. My heart ached.

The baby was in the nursery getting her bath. Today, I waited a little while and decided to walk to the nursery to see how my little Peanut was doing. As I opened the double doors to the nursery, I couldn't believe my eyes. There he was looking through the glass window, staring at our little angel. The nurse was holding her up to the window so he could get a closer look. He looked at me and smiled.

"She is amazing, just like her mother, Kid. I didn't know if I should have come, but I had to see the baby. I hope you don't mind." I could feel my heart pounding in my chest.

"No, it's fine, Jake. I don't mind at all. I'm glad you came."

Epilogue

I was sitting at the bar nursing my third whiskey. I had received a call from Emma's father.

She was in labor. Why? What would be the purpose? There was no reason for me to go to the hospital, he said. She just wanted me to know the baby was coming.

This did not go the way I had planned, not at all. Being knocked unconscious, the amnesia, and especially not the baby. But there is a baby, and it could be mine. That changed everything for me. She wanted the baby to be Jake's, and that's the way I was going to let it be. I wasn't going to get in her way. I could feel a lump swell in my throat. I took another drink.

I wished I could go back all these months and change things. Things I had set in motion without Emma even knowing she was part of my plot.

I had an appointment with a Dr. James Farrell; we were to discuss my post-traumatic stress disorder. I really didn't want to go and spill my guts to some stranger, but it was all part of my rehabilitation. I didn't want to take medication to numb my mental and physical pain either. That wouldn't change what I witnessed or had done. I walked into his office and sat in a leather club chair. Nice office. He sat opposite me in the same chair with a pad and pen. Obviously, this doctor was doing very well for himself. He asked me some questions about my military life, personal life, and I gave him quick, simple answers.

While I looked around the office, I noticed a picture on his desk. Pretty woman, sweet face. He was obviously older than the woman in the picture. He was a lucky man. It had to be his wife. He was wearing a wedding band. I looked at the smiling face in the picture again. I would like to have some of what Doc here is having. What were the chances of me meeting his pretty little wife?

I obviously kept my thoughts to myself, of course. Then getting off the elevator, who should I run into but, and I mean literally run into, the pretty little Mrs. Farrell. It was very obvious she was attracted to me. It was all over her flushed face. Why not take the chance of running into her again? I formed a plan. I would wait outside the building after my appointment the following week. She might come to the office and meet her husband again. And sure enough, on Friday around six thirty, there she was, standing in front of the building.

She looked like she was waiting for someone, but it didn't appear to be Jake. She kept watching the homeless man, with his dog, in front of the building. You could see she was truly upset by this person. Eventually, she put money in his paper cup, pet the dog, and walked away. If she was waiting for someone, they didn't show. I followed her, and when she stopped at the corner to hail a cab, I took my chances. I started talking to her. She obviously remembered me, and it worked. I could really fall for this woman. I could see she was totally attracted to me. I set my plan in motion. I convinced her to have a drink with me, and it began from there. I thought she was falling for me the way I was falling for her. It was something in the way she made love to me. It made me feel almost human again.

There was something about the way she looked at me. I wanted to have someone like her in my life. I never let on that her husband was my psychiatrist, which would have ruined my plan. She never mentioned him, so that made it all the easier for me. I even went along with her telling me her name was Liz Flynn. I knew full well it was Emma Farrell. If it meant being with her, I'll call her Liz.

She could be the love I never let myself experience before. I even tried hiding her heart in my apartment when I removed her wet top and it fell from her neck. I knew she would have to come back for it. She would be here on Saturday. I couldn't wait till Saturday.

I should have stayed home that night and not gone out for a drink. I saw the girl in the bar sitting next to me leave and a few minutes later heard screams from outside. She was being attacked. I just couldn't let it go. It wasn't like me to just stand by. That's when everything went wrong; the attack, the amnesia, and not remembering Liz. Imagine Dr. Farrell trying to help me remember who Liz was, all along not knowing it was his beloved wife I was sleeping with.

And then, the kindhearted psychiatrist took me to his apartment for a home-cooked dinner. Liz was wearing the heart that hung in my face as we made love. She sipped the white wine as she did the first night we spoke in the bar and went to my place.

Then hearing the rain beating against the windows, and the claps of thunder, the memories of her standing in my apartment soaking wet, all came flooding back. She saw the look on my face as I left the Farrells' apartment. She knew I remembered her. She said nothing. She knew she had no recourse. One day, she would have to tell Jake.

After my dinner with Emma and Jake, I cordially asked him how his lovely wife was doing at my following session. He told me she went to their cottage to rest; she was expecting and was feeling a little rundown. She needed some quiet time, and I would guess some time away from me too. Could it be he still had no idea about us? He must be a little suspicious after our awkward dinner the other night. She still hadn't told him. But I knew she would have to someday. I needed to find out if the baby was mine.

I went to see her at the cottage. I could see that she didn't want to hurt me, but she had no choice. I thought maybe she would want to be with me. I could be part of her and the baby's lives. I could have tried hard to make a good life with them. I never could before, but now things were different. I was home for good. I wanted a new life. I knew she was married; she loved Jake. Why did I even try? What was I thinking? I just needed a woman, a lover, a friend. I wasn't thinking straight. I'm still not.

I went home and sat on my couch looking at my bed remembering.

My cell phone buzzed. I answered, and a soft voice spoke, "Hello, is this Ethan? Dr. Harris gave me your phone number. I know it's been a while. My name is Darcy. I never had the chance to thank you for what you did for me that night...

CPSIA information can be obtained
at www.ICGtesting.com
Printed in the USA
BVHW071124011121
620451BV00001B/110

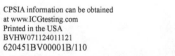